A Heart Never Dies

KAREN G. BRUCE

Jan-Carol
Publishing, Inc

"every story needs a book"

A Heart Never Dies
Written by Karen G. Bruce

Published February 2023
Little Creek Books
Imprint of Jan-Carol Publishing, Inc.
All rights reserved
Copyright © 2023 Karen G. Bruce

ISBN: 978-1-954978-78-2
Library of Congress Control Number: 2023931999

You may contact the publisher:
Jan-Carol Publishing, Inc.
PO Box 701
Johnson City, TN 37605
publisher@jancarolpublishing.com
www.jancarolpublishing.com

I would like to dedicate this book to my mother, Wanda Sheppard.

She's my biggest fan and biggest supporter.

I love you, Mama.

"Goodbyes are only for those who love with their eyes. Because for those who love with heart and soul there is no such thing as separation."

— RUMI

Chapter 1

Jenna buried her husband on a Monday afternoon. A light rain was falling, and by the evidence of the vapor of breath in front of her face, she knew it must be cold. Jenna didn't feel the cold—only numbness. A sea of sad, pinched faces greeted her wherever she turned. People spoke to her, but she didn't hear them. She really didn't want to hear them. She knew they meant well, but did they think anything they had to say would make it better? Would their empty words bring Craig back? Would their '*I'm so sorrys*' mend her broken heart?

Jenna's mom patted her on the leg, giving her the '*If anyone understands, it's me*' look. Jenna was sick of that look. She loved her mom, but sometimes she couldn't breathe around her. Elizabeth Johnston was the authority on everything, or thought she was anyway. Her observations and advice usually ended with, "You follow?" Jenna and her best friend, Rachel, would always imitate her mom and follow with the inevitable clucking sound, head tilted, and one eyebrow raised for added effect.

Jenna's mother leaned in and whispered, "Take deep breaths, dear. You'll hyperventilate if you're not careful. It will come on you before you know it. You follow?" Cluck, cluck.

Jenna lost her father when she was 12 years old. He had been complaining of a severe headache, which turned out to be a brain aneurysm, and he had died within a week. If Elizabeth grieved at all, it was in private. Typical of that generation, Frank had been hard working, spending long hours every day in the office or on the road selling insurance. Jenna loved her father but never saw him much, so his passing wasn't all that noticeable for her. She did remember him opening her door every night and telling her goodnight and whispering that he loved her. He always seemed so tired. In the end, he took care of his wife by leaving her a nice, hefty insurance policy that allowed her to continue her volunteer work and to take care of their only daughter.

Jenna thought of her own daughter. Abby, 16, was a carbon copy of Jenna and had been the light of Craig's life. How in the world would they make it without him? Surely this was all a bad dream, and she would eventually wake up. Craig would laugh at her, saying, "I'm never going to leave you, baby. You're stuck with me for life." Jenna smiled through the haze. Yes, it's just a nightmare, a horrible, horrible nightmare.

Jenna jumped when she heard her daughter's sob, jerking her back into reality. Abby's shoulders were slumped and her whole body was trembling. Suddenly, her daughter jumped up and ran out from under the protection of the funeral tent. Jenna watched helplessly as Abby stumbled toward the black limousine the funeral home provided for these somber occasions. Katy, Abby's best friend, followed right behind her. Not caring about anyone else, Jenna jumped up too, but her mother grabbed the back of her dress and wouldn't let go.

"Let her be."

Jenna watched as an employee from the funeral home held an umbrella and opened the car door so Abby and Katy could get out of the rain. Was he expecting them? Did that happen a lot? He stood there stoically like he worked for the National Guard instead of the Kiser Funeral Home.

Jenna shivered and then peeked at her husband's casket. It was silver, just like his pick-up truck. He had bought "Bullet" two years ago because of his promotion at work. She remembered how happy he was when he was named the new head football coach at Cramer High School.

The school was in Cramerton, a small town close to Charlotte, North Carolina. Even though it meant he would spend more time away from his family, Jenna was happy for him because she knew it was his dream. "Bullet" was nothing but a mangled mess now. The night his team won their sixth straight game, Craig never made it home. A drunk driver was driving on the wrong side of the road and hit Craig head on. Craig lay in a coma, brain dead, for three days. Jenna finally worked up the courage to remove him from life support and let him die. The drunk driver lived with just a couple of broken bones to show for his complete lack of judgment.

Jenna looked around and saw a sea of umbrellas around the tent. Even though it was raining, people were everywhere. Craig would have scoffed at that, wondering why they would stand in the rain, mourning him. She could just hear him saying, "Don't cry for me! Go home and hug someone and tell them that you love them!" There wasn't a day that went by that Craig hadn't told her he loved her. He always made sure that the people he loved knew it. "Love ya, mean it" was his catch phrase. The secretaries in the front office loved him, his team loved him, and his students loved him. Everyone loved Craig and his vibrant personality. He never met a stranger, while Jenna was quieter and more reserved. He had taught high school health and P.E., and Jenna was the media center director at the middle school.

They had met at a college party during their freshman year at Appalachian State University. Dragged there by her roommate, Chrissie, Jenna was sitting on a grungy couch, bored to tears, wishing she was back in her dorm room reading. That's when Craig sat down next to her. He put his arm around her and whispered, "Can you pretend you're my girlfriend so this crazy lunatic will leave me alone?" Jenna looked up and saw the 'crazy lunatic' giving them both the evil eye, hands on her hips. Jenna then looked at Craig and his pleading eyes and slowly nodded, trying not to grin but failing miserably.

She had seen Craig before and actually had a little bit of a crush on him, as did most of the freshmen girls. He had blonde hair that had a hint of copper highlights. He was a quarterback on the football team but was average height and build. Her heart began racing when he took her hand in his. In her ear he whispered, "I'm going to kiss you, okay?" Jenna's heart stopped as his lips softly touched hers. Something magical happened when they kissed that night, causing them both to look at each other in total wonder. The next kiss happened as if they were two magnets, and they only parted when someone yelled, "Get a room!" They both jumped back in amazement, stunned by what had just happened.

Jenna was speechless but Craig said, "Did you just feel what I felt?" causing her to grin and bite her lip. "Who are you, anyway? I definitely haven't seen you around."

Jenna cocked her head and said, "Apparently, I'm your new girlfriend. By the way, I never kiss on the first date."

Craig grinned and said, "Too late. I think if you're going to be my new girlfriend, I should at least know your name."

"Jenna."

She looked down and realized Craig was still holding her hand. His thumb was absently rubbing circles in the center of her palm. She felt every nerve tingle and in a good way.

"Hi, Jenna." He had this ridiculous grin on his face, causing Jenna to smile back in that goofy, shy way. "I'm Craig Rogers, and I think I'm in love."

Jenna, lost in her thoughts, jumped when everyone began standing up. Apparently, the service was over, and she realized she hadn't heard a word the preacher said. Judging by the tears on everyone's faces, they were moved. Craig had been a beloved member of the community, and his loss would be felt for a long time.

Regardless of the nasty weather, well-meaning people kept coming up to her and offering their condolences. Tired, old phrases kept popping up. "He's in a better place." "You're in our thoughts and prayers." "Coach Rogers will never be forgotten." She nodded and smiled like she was supposed to. Soon it would be over. Soon she would be in her bed with the covers over her head.

Rachel and Elizabeth walked with Jenna to the car while somebody held an umbrella over their heads. Jenna could feel her sensible black pumps squishing in the cold, wet grass. Shaking, she scooted into the seat of the limo and saw Abby's red, swollen eyes. Holding out her arms, Abby fell into them and they both cried for what seemed like an eternity. Jenna tried to comfort her only child; all that she had left of Craig. Abby had been Craig's pride and joy. There was nothing he wouldn't do for her, including tea parties, shopping, or being a guinea pig for beauty makeovers. Craig did it all and did it enthusiastically. The big football coach was nothing but a softie when it came to Abigail Louisa Rogers, or as he liked to call her, "Abby Lou Lou."

Once home, Jenna and Abby escaped to their rooms. Rachel was probably in the kitchen making sure all the food was set up and ready to go. She had been there as soon as she found out about Craig, comforting Jenna and Abby. Rachel was a math teacher at the same middle school where Jenna worked, and they had been best friends for 10 years. Jenna had helped Rachel when she was diagnosed with breast cancer and stood by her, especially when her husband decided it was too much for him to deal with. Rachel lost her breasts and husband but not her life.

The small three-bedroom ranch home already felt cramped and overrun with well-wishers. Jenna knew this was all part of the death experience, but she couldn't help but feel resentful. Why couldn't they all just leave and go home? All she wanted was to be left alone, with only Craig's memories to keep her company. She would close her eyes and pretend that he was lying there beside her. That was the only comfort she wanted and needed.

Curling up on Craig's side of the bed, Jenna hugged his pillow close. She was so cold. Would she ever feel warm again? Willing herself to sleep, Jenna pretended Craig's arms were around her, whispering in her ear that everything would be okay. He would tell her one of his ridiculous jokes and make her laugh. He loved to make her laugh.

"Jenna! Wake up." Jenna's mother was gently shaking her shoulders. "Honey, you have to get up."

"But I don't want to." Jenna curled up even tighter and spoke into the pillow. "Just thank everyone for me and tell them that I'm just not up for company. Please, Mom, I can't do this anymore. I'm exhausted." Jenna thought that she had effectively dismissed her, but apparently her mom had other ideas.

"Absolutely not. Go splash some water on your face and cover up your dark circles." Elizabeth clucked and put her hands on her hips. "When your father died, I didn't want to come out of my room either, but I did. I didn't want to live my life without him, but I did. God gave me strength, and he'll give it to you, too."

Jenna thought about arguing with her. Where was God when Craig got hit by that stupid drunk driver? Why did Craig die and not him? She wanted to argue but knew it was useless. Her mother had an answer for everything.

Taking a deep breath, Jenna nodded. With determination and something akin to anger, she got up and headed toward the bathroom. "Fine, but I can tell you right now that if they're not gone soon, you better tell them to leave, or I will." Turning around, she stormed into the bathroom, gasping when she saw her red, swollen eyes and tear-stained face. Turning on the hot water, she let it run until it was almost scalding, placing her washcloth under it until it was soaked. Taking the hot cloth to her face felt good. She promised herself that she would take a hot bath later. Maybe that would warm her up. Craig used to laugh at her when she took long hot baths because, afterward, her backside would be as red as a lobster. She never understood why, but he always took cold showers. He said it energized him. It must have been true because he was always annoyingly hyper in the mornings, especially next to her sluggish, grumpy self. She couldn't wait to get that first cup of coffee to help wake her up.

After running a brush through her hair and dabbing on some makeup concealer, Jenna took a deep breath and prayed for strength. "Okay, God, do your thing because I'm going to fall apart at any moment." She opened her bedroom door and walked down the hallway, noticing Abby's room was empty. Seeing her mother waiting on her in the den, Jenna asked, "Where's Abby?"

With her arms crossed and lips pursed, Elizabeth said, "Isaac is here. They went outside for a walk." Elizabeth was old school and didn't approve of Abby dating a boy of a different color. Craig had not been happy that Abby was dating Isaac either, but for a different reason. Isaac was a couple of years older than her. He didn't want anyone to date his little girl, but finally relented when Abby turned 16.

Isaac had been one of Craig's varsity football players. He was smart and handsome, and Jenna could see why Abby liked him. The only fault Jenna had with Isaac was his own family's lack of discipline. Isaac could stay out late and do pretty much whatever he wanted. His parents were both lawyers and worked long hours, leaving Isaac and his younger brother on their own much of the time.

Jenna nodded and looked around the room. She saw Craig's mother sitting in the recliner. She recognized that faraway look in her eyes. Walking over to her, she knelt down and took her hand. "Hey, Lynn, you okay?"

Lynn shook her head, trying not to cry. "Not really. Maybe I will be when I can make some kind of sense of all of this. Did you know that driver already had two drunk-driving tickets? How could they let someone like that on the road? What's this world coming to?"

Jenna squeezed her hand and said, "I don't know, Lynn, but if I found him, I believe I could kill him with my own bare hands."

"You and me both, honey, you and me both."

Chapter 2

Time was ticking for Benjamin Thompson. He was normally upbeat and positive, but lately it was getting harder and harder. He tried not to dwell on the past year because it only made him feel depressed, which didn't help his situation. According to his doctors, his heart was failing fast, and his only hope was the miracle of a new one. Knowing that someone had to die so that he could live wasn't fair. That was why he was preparing himself to die. He knew someone was out there, more deserving than him.

Since Sarah left him, it wasn't that hard to just give up. She said she left him because she loved him so much that she couldn't just watch him die. Whatever the reason, it hurt like nothing had ever hurt before. And to think, it really hadn't been that long ago when he thought he had it all.

He thought about Sarah and their marriage. He had fallen in love with her when they met five years ago. She was so beautiful and young, too young according to his mother. She had warned him, had wondered what they had in common, but Ben couldn't see beyond the long, blonde hair that fell down her back in waves or the legs that seemed to go on forever. He loved her smile, her sweet personality, and her abundance of energy. They had met at the gym, and he would never forget the first time he saw her running on the treadmill. He couldn't believe it when she actually spoke to him, pulling him into a conversation about yoga.

She couldn't talk enough about yoga. At first, he thought she was just a chatterbox like his mother, so he avoided her. But the more he avoided her, the more she pursued him, and then he was hooked.

She was a public relations representative for Belmont University. He was an engineer for an architectural firm and graduated from the same university almost 15 years before she did. He began to look forward to seeing her at the gym every day, but of course, he wasn't the only one. She was never without someone to talk to, but amazingly Sarah always made a point to include him in whatever silly conversation she was having. He couldn't believe his luck when she asked him to go running with her on a Saturday morning. He finally got up the courage to ask her on a date, and when she said yes, he knew that his dreams were coming true. Unfortunately, it wasn't a good dream, it was a nightmare.

Ben had dated a lot of women over the years, but very few made a lasting impression. He got bored quickly or found something lacking in their looks or personality. There was always something that caused him to move on, and there were a couple of hearts that got broken along the way. Now Ben was on the receiving end of a broken heart, in more ways than one. The woman that was perfect in every way left him when the going got tough.

Ben guessed that trying to keep up with Sarah and her energetic lifestyle is what finally did him in. He never knew that his heart was defective until he went to the doctor because of his constant fatigue. The doctors told him he was lucky that he hadn't already had a massive heart attack. Ben wondered if that would have been better—better than lying around, waiting for someone to die. The odds were against him anyway. Finding a perfect match was nearly impossible.

Now he was in the hospital and his days were numbered. He couldn't stand to see the pity in his mom's face. Ben's own father had died when he was just 40 years old. He had a massive heart attack, leaving a young wife and two children. Ben's sister, Laura, was a couple of years younger and lived across the country. Sarah hadn't been to see him in months.

It would be so easy to just close his eyes and give up. The divorce was already final. What did he really have to live for?

"What are you thinking about, Benji?" Nancy, his mother, sat next to his hospital bed quietly crocheting a baby blanket for someone at church.

He felt guilty and hoped she didn't know how hopeless he felt. "I'm just so tired, Mom. I wish things were different."

"Oh, Benji, don't give up. You've got to stay positive. You never know what God has planned for you." She patted his hand, bringing it to her lips.

Ben sighed. "Well, if it's anything like the past year, he must not like me very much."

Squeezing his hand, she said, "Now, cut it out. You have so much to be thankful for. At least you have a chance to get better once you get a new heart. Your life will be brand new, and nothing will be impossible." Nancy's faith was immense, and the thought never crossed her mind that finding a new heart was just about hopeless.

He never would have made it this long without her. Even though she warned him that Sarah wasn't right for him, she never once bad-mouthed her. She was always there for him and was his one and only advocate. Ben smiled and used what energy he had to squeeze her hand back.

"Besides, young man, I'm still waiting on that grandchild."

His sister, Laura, was in the movie industry and had no interest in children. Nancy had never been silent about her wish for grandbabies. Children were the last thing on Ben's list of things to accomplish right now, survival being on the top of the list. Also, in the back of his mind was the little matter of a heart defect and the fact that he would more than likely pass it on to his own children. In his mind, it would be too big of a risk. If he did receive the miracle of a new heart, children would not be in his future, but he couldn't tell his mother that. He refused to dwell on it because it probably wouldn't matter anyway.

"Mom, I need you to do something for me." His mom looked expectantly at him, waiting for his plea as if it was the most important request of his life. "I need you to call Brittany at work and ask her what I need to do to change the beneficiary of my insurance policy from Sarah to you."

His mom sat forward and put her blanket down. "Oh, for heaven's sake, Benji, you're not going anywhere." She picked up her crochet needle again and began working her hands furiously.

"But if I do, I don't want Sarah to get a penny of that life insurance. Would you just do it and not argue about it?" He knew his mother could certainly use the money even if she wouldn't admit it.

"I'll call your secretary tomorrow to see what you need to do, but it will embarrass me to death to ask about money." When Ben continued to look at his mother, she sighed. "I'll do it because I don't want you to worry about it." She stood up and placed her unfinished blanket on the chair. "Now, you rest while I head down to the cafeteria and get some coffee."

Ben nodded and watched her leave the room. He'd give anything to have enough energy to get up out of the bed and go with her. Just having a regular conversation wore him out. Ben closed his eyes and gave in to the ever-present fatigue. Maybe this was it. Maybe he would go to sleep and never wake up. He was so tired of being tired all the time. He really didn't mind dying except for knowing his mom would be sad. He was saved and baptized in church when he was 14 years old and went to the altar a couple more times after that just to be on the safe side. God promised if he believed in Jesus he would go to heaven when he died. The chlorinated water in the baptismal pool washed his sins away, so he was good to go. He was thinking of the sins of his teenage self as he drifted off to sleep.

A flurry of activity in his hospital room woke Ben up. He heard snippets of conversation including, "Get him to the operating room, STAT!" His mom was crying, "It's a miracle! My prayers have been answered!" Before he knew it, they were wheeling him down the hallway, and that was the last thing he remembered.

Chapter 3

Jenna stood in her closet smelling Craig's shirts. Most of his clothing had the colors of Cramer High School; purple and silver. She had on one of his sweatshirts, trying to keep the cold away, and also hoping she would feel closer to him by wearing it. It smelled of him still. She and Abby were going through the motions, but it wasn't getting any easier, not for her anyway. Abby had already returned to school, and Jenna was supposed to report back to work the following Monday. Could she do it? Everyone said the first day is the hardest and it would get easier after that. What if she broke down and cried like a baby all day? What good would she be? She wished she could stay home and become a hermit, reading and drinking coffee all day long.

It had been two weeks since Officer Sproles broke the news that would change her life forever. Tom Sproles was the resource officer at the high school and a good friend of Craig's. Jenna would never forget the look on his face when he told her about the wreck. She couldn't imagine how hard that must have been for him. They both cried.

Jenna walked out of the closet and sat down on the bed. Falling back, she stared at the ceiling while tears rolled down each side of her face. She knew there was nothing she could have done to prevent the accident that killed Craig, but she still felt guilty somehow. Things were so hectic after the game that night, and she didn't even get to say *congratulations, goodbye,* or *see you when you get home.* Nothing! Now it was too late. He would never know how proud she was.

Jenna rolled over on her side, trying to fight the pain that engulfed her whole body. Not being able to say goodbye was the worst feeling in the world. When she could stand it no more, the wrenching sobs began. *I'm so sorry, Craig! I wish I could tell you how much you meant to me!* Jenna felt something rubbing against her and realized it was Chip.

Chocolate Chip or "Chip" for short, because of his silky dark brown and white fur, was Craig's cat. He found him hanging out at the school's dumpsters last year, nearly on death's door. He brought him home much to Jenna's dismay. She didn't like animals in the house, not to mention having cat fur everywhere and a stinky litter box to clean up. She gave in, feeling sorry for Chip, and because she could never say no to Craig. She remembered Craig holding up the mangy scrap of a cat with huge yellow eyes that were crusty and scared. "Just look at that face. I'll take him to Dr. Hovis, and he'll fix him right up."

Fortunately, Chip turned out to be a great pet. Abby was crazy about him, and he made himself an important part of the family in a very short time. Jenna pulled Chip close to her, and his steady purr seemed to soothe her frayed nerves. He nuzzled her neck as if he was trying to give her comfort at a time when she needed it the most. Jenna smiled through her tears, knowing that Craig was there with her somehow. *I love you, Craig. I miss you so much.* Somehow, she knew that Craig could hear her and felt some smidgen of peace because of it. Maybe she would survive. Maybe one day she could live again.

Jenna heard the front door slam and jumped. The noise spooked Chip, and he jumped down.

"Mom!" Wiping her eyes quickly, Jenna stood up and walked towards the bedroom door, but Abby opened it before she got there. "Mom, can I go to a Halloween party tonight? It's at Miranda Hollister's house. Isaac can take me there and bring me home. Please?"

Halloween? Jenna had forgotten all about Halloween! Maybe she would turn out all the lights and pretend nobody was home. Jenna quickly dismissed the idea, knowing that Craig would have a cow if he found out she didn't hand out candy. It was one of his favorite holidays. If he was lucky enough to be home, he never missed a chance to greet every kid that rang the doorbell. He would grill every trick-or-treater with question after question and then finally give them a huge handful of candy. One, or even two pieces, was never enough. Her heart broke again, knowing he would never see another Halloween, Thanksgiving, or Christmas. No more birthdays, Valentines, or Fourth of Julys. He loved the holidays, had always looked for an excuse to decorate or throw a party.

"Mom, can I go?"

"I don't know, honey, why don't you just stay here with me and hand out candy? We could order pizza." Jenna could hear the pathetic whine in her voice and cringed. Grabbing Abby's upper arms she said, "Never mind, you go and you have a good time, just please be careful."

"Are you sure you'll be okay?"

Jenna smiled, trying to reassure her. Abby had enough on her mind without having to worry about her mother. "Of course I will. Anyway, I have a ton of things to get done before I go back to work Monday. Please don't worry about me. I'll probably call Rachel and see if she wants to come over." Seeing her daughter's reluctance, Jenna tried to change the subject. "Are you going to dress up?"

"I don't know. It's kind of like a last-minute thing. Isaac's not into dressing up; not like..." Abby's face drained of all color and big, fat tears filled her eyes.

Jenna pulled her into her arms. "Oh, honey, please don't cry."

"But Halloween was one of Dad's favorite holidays," Abby sobbed. "I miss him so much!"

They both cried until Jenna took her daughter's hand and led her to the living room. "How about a cup of tea? Nothing makes you feel better than a cup of jasmine tea with honey." As Jenna busied herself putting the tea kettle on to boil in the kitchen, Abby curled up on the sofa and pulled the fleece blanket up around her. Chip jumped up in her lap and began purring and kneading the blanket.

When the tea was done, Jenna handed a cup to Abby and then sat down next to her, her hands wrapped around the warm mug. "Remember that time when your dad dressed up like a ghost and that little boy got scared and punched him in his privates?" Jenna smiled. "I didn't think he would ever get his deep voice back."

Abby laughed. "Yeah, that was hilarious. He put a sports cup on after that and said, 'You live and learn!'" She was silent for a moment and then said, "Mom, do you ever, like, wish that you could predict the future so you might do things differently?"

"What do you mean?" Jenna noticed that Abby's lip was beginning to quiver. "What, Abby, what happened?"

Abby sniffed and then took a deep breath. "The day Dad died I, like, did something. I think I hurt his feelings." She looked at her mom, pain apparent in her eyes. "I asked him if I could go with Isaac and his family to their cabin in the mountains to see the fall colors. Dad said, 'Absolutely not.'"

"What did you say?"

"I yelled like a two-year-old and told him it wasn't fair, and that was the last time I spoke to him." Between hiccups, she sobbed. "Oh, Mom! Why did I have to be such a baby?"

Jenna pulled Abby into her arms.

"Honey, you know your dad. He probably didn't think a thing about it. He knew you would get over it and be fine. I guarantee you he wasn't mad or hurt. I know one thing though; he would be hurt if he knew how upset and worried you were about it now." Jenna rubbed Abby's back until her sobs subsided. "Now drink your tea; you'll feel better."

They sat in silence for a moment until Abby said, "Do you ever, like, wonder who got Dad's heart?"

Jenna sucked in her breath. That was something she really couldn't think about yet. Knowing that there may be someone with Craig's beating heart, his lifeblood, gave her chills. He had insisted that if something ever happened to him, his organs be donated to someone who needed them. When the doctor approached her in the hospital about donating his organs, Jenna was hardly aware of anything, much less the seriousness of his organs going into someone else's body. She looked at her daughter and smiled. "I don't know, Abby. Whoever it was got the best part of him."

Chapter 4

N ancy Thompson watched her son fade in and out of consciousness for days. She knew it was only a matter of time before he woke up and then walked out of the hospital. It was touch and go for a while, but her faith never wavered. The doctors kept warning her that his body may reject the new heart, but she just ignored them. Nancy was a prayer warrior and she had connections with other prayer warriors. Prayers could do miracles, and that's exactly what Benji needed. She wasn't impressed with the church she had attended for years, so she joined a new church. This church family lifted Benji up, and she had no doubts that he would pull through and eventually live the life he was meant to live.

Nancy stretched out her arthritic fingers. She had crocheted so much in the last few weeks that her fingers were becoming stiff and sore. Her knuckles were swollen and red, but she couldn't stop. What else was she going to do while sitting in the hospital day after day? Sitting at home wasn't an option. She wanted to be there the second Benji opened his eyes. She had kept his sister, Laura, up to date faithfully, but Nancy couldn't understand why she wouldn't take the time to come and see Benji for herself. Laura said there wasn't anything she could do anyway, that she would rather visit when she could actually spend quality time with her brother.

Nancy loved both of her children equally, but Benji had a special place in her heart. He was sweet and thoughtful, while Laura could argue with a saint. Ever since she was a little girl, Laura had been too smart for her own good. She was just like Ed's mother, bless her heart. Myrtle Thompson was bossy and had Ed and all of her children under her thumb until the day she died. Laura even looked like Myrtle, big bosom and all.

Nancy picked up her phone to see what time it was and then looked at her son. Benji was having a good day today. Yesterday was a different story. She shivered just thinking of the close call he had. The nurses wouldn't tell her much, but the doctors were concerned about a possible rejection. Nancy just prayed harder. She didn't think about *if* Benji survived but about when he would leave the hospital and live the life he was supposed to live; one that would bring her a grandchild. Her friend, Vera, already had five grandchildren. Surely God would give her at least one little baby to spoil before she got too old.

Every time Vera showed pictures and videos of her grandchildren, Nancy made sure she *oohed* and *ah'd* and exclaimed how wonderful, smart, and funny they all were, all the time thinking 'When *am I ever going to have grandchildren?*' She tried not to be jealous, but secretly she was, although she would never admit it to Vera. She asked for the Lord's forgiveness each night for coveting someone else's blessings. There was still hope for Benji. Although he said he didn't want children because he didn't want to pass down his own heart defect, Nancy prayed that he would change his mind. Laura was adamant that she didn't want children. Nancy couldn't understand why they didn't have the desire to have children of their own. They had no idea what they were missing. Raising Laura and Benji had been Nancy's greatest accomplishment in life. The hardest part was letting them go.

Nancy looked at her son sleeping peacefully. There wasn't a day that went by that she didn't burst with pride for Benji and Laura. They were both smart, hard-working, and kind. Laura was a little headstrong and sassy but that was the way God made her. Nancy was proud that Laura spoke up for herself and was a strong woman. She did worry about her faith. Laura and Benji were both saved and baptized when they were teens, but Laura didn't live that life anymore. *Things were different in California*, she said. *There's not a Baptist church on every street, and people look at you funny when you talk about Jesus*, she tried to explain to her mom. Nancy was careful and tried not to say the wrong thing. She tried to be *gentle*, just like Paul said in the New Testament, but so far it wasn't working. Every night she prayed that Laura would have a deeper relationship with God, that God would send someone in her life that would help her realize that.

Nancy closed her eyes, saying a short prayer, thanking God for all he had done for Benji. His doctor was a Christian and even prayed with Nancy. He told her that Benji had a rough road ahead of him, but he had every confidence that he would live a full, productive life. When she opened her eyes, Benji was staring at her.

Chapter 5

"What do you mean she's not at school?"

Jenna had two classes in the Media Center, and it was packed. Kids were doing more socializing than anything while some were reading the periodicals, which wouldn't be any help for the book reports they were supposed to be working on. People magazine and Teen magazine didn't contain anything about American authors, and she tried to tell them that, but all she got back were snickers and a bunch of eye rolling. Personally, Jenna felt like a babysitter or the phone police most of the time.

"Was she there this morning?"

The assistant principal at Abby's school informed Jenna that Abby had reported to first period but not second or third.

"Okay, I'll see if I can find out what's going on."

Jenna hung up and immediately called Abby's cell, which went straight to voicemail. She tried to find her location on an app but it was 'unavailable.' Frustrated, she took a deep breath and wondered where in the world her daughter might be. The first person she thought of was Isaac. Jenna called his cell, and when it went straight to voicemail, her heart dropped. *Great! Now what am I going to do?*

She had 10 more minutes until the period ended. Once the students left, she would put a CLOSED sign on the Media Center door and send emails to the teachers to cancel further activities for the day. She wanted to head home to see if Abby was there. Whatever Abby's reason for leaving school without permission would not be acceptable. Lately, Abby seemed to be getting more and more belligerent. Jenna had her own problems to deal with, and she didn't need her daughter pushing her at every turn. Sometimes she just wanted to throw up her hands and give up. Craig would know what to do, but of course he wasn't here, thanks to some stupid drunk driver.

Officer Sproles found out that the man who had caused the accident was already out of jail. He lost his license, but he would probably be back out on the road again in no time with or without a license. He needed to be in court-mandated rehab for alcoholism. He also needed a quick kick in the butt, and Jenna would gladly be the person to volunteer for the job. Oh, if she could just get her hands on him! Now that reality had set in, Jenna was mad all the time. She was mad at everyone—including Craig. How could he leave her when she needed him now more than ever? He always knew how to deal with Abby; she had been putty in his hands. Jenna only seemed to make everything worse. Whatever she said to Abby was the wrong thing. They had clung to each other at first, glad to have each other to lean on. Jenna felt as if everything was slipping through her fingers now. Her daughter was so headstrong and stubborn.

As Jenna pulled in the driveway, she pushed the button to open the garage door. Abby's car was parked inside so she pulled up beside it and turned off the engine. She could hear the music blaring from inside before she even entered the house. With her heart in her stomach, she opened the door and walked in. As she reached Abby's closed bedroom door, she took a breath and slowly turned the doorknob knowing that whatever she found inside was not going to be good. The sight that greeted her was enough to make her throw up. Isaac's naked body covered her daughter, and there was no doubt about what they were doing. Abby's pink and white comforter was pushed down to the foot of the bed, half of it lying on the carpet. It was worse than not good; it was horrible and revolting and Jenna was disturbed to her very core.

All she could do was scream. "Abby!" Abby raised her head in panic, pushing Isaac from her body. They both scrambled, trying to pull the blanket up to cover themselves. Their eyes were wide open revealing absolute horror and dread. Jenna covered her face with her hand in complete shock. "What? What? Oh my word." She must have said *oh my word* at least 10 times before she finally hung her head. *Please tell me this is not happening. Please let this be a dream.*

Abby was crying softly, "I'm sorry, Mom."

Jenna wanted to scream and stomp her feet in frustration. She knew it would hurt Abby, but she said it anyway because she could not stop the words coming out of her mouth. She wanted Abby to feel the same hurt that she did. "Do you know how disappointed your father would be right now? His heart would be broken!"

"Thanks a lot, Mom," Abby said pathetically and then hung her head, crying softly. Next to her, Isaac was looking down, his hands covering his face.

"You need to leave now, Isaac." Jenna turned her back so he could put his clothes on. "I never want to see your face around here again. You hear me? Ever! Don't ever!"

Isaac tried to apologize to Jenna, but she wasn't having any of it. "Just get out Isaac! I can't, I just can't!"

"Mrs. Rogers, I'm really sorry but I don't have my car. Can I call..."

Jenna cut him off by screaming, "Do you think I care? You can walk home. You've got 10 seconds before I call the police. You are 18, right? Ever hear of statutory rape?"

Knowing it was fruitless, Isaac gave Abby one last look and then turned and practically ran out the door once he was partially dressed. Jenna watched him run down the hallway, and then she looked back at her daughter. "Now get dressed, Abby. We obviously need to talk. I'll be in the living room."

Jenna walked out of Abby's bedroom and to the living room where she sat down on the couch. Bright, warm sunshine was pouring through the windows, calling attention to dust particles floating in the air. Jenna looked at the popcorn ceiling above and whispered, "God, please help me." Chip meandered his way to the couch and then hopped up next to her, rubbing the side of his head on her leg. He slowly got on her lap and began kneading her chest. Jenna closed her eyes and leaned back on the couch. Even though it was a warm day for November, Jenna felt the cold all the way to her bones.

Jenna heard Abby walk in the living room and opened one eye as she sat down on the opposite side of the couch. Her daughter's head was down, and her bottom lip stuck out, reminding Jenna of when she was a little girl. All she had to do was put out that bottom lip and Craig was hooked. He always had an excuse if she was naughty. The teacher deserved it (when Abby was caught sticking her tongue out when she made some remark about her constant jabbering) or she was just hungry (when Abby snuck and ate a whole bag of powdered sugar donuts before dinner) or she was just being silly (when Abby sang *beans, beans good for your heart, the more you eat the more you fart* to her Sunday School class). Jenna wasn't so gullible. *See what happens when your little girl grows up thinking she can do anything she wants to, Craig? Now you're gone and I'm left with the consequences!*

Jenna couldn't believe that her 16-year-old daughter was already having sex. When she was that age, it was the last thing on her mind. Heck, she wasn't even really sure what sex meant back then. Jenna and Craig didn't have sex until their senior year in college, but not for lack of trying on Craig's part. She told him over and over she wanted to wait until they were married, but one night she got tired of waiting, too. They had finished their exams before winter break and celebrated by ordering a pizza. They were at Jenna's apartment. Her three roommates had already gone home for the holiday. They had the opened box of pizza on the couch between them, and their feet were propped up on the coffee table. Jenna had picked up the last piece and held it above her head, dangling it above her mouth. "Whoever invented pizza was a genius—a genius I tell you!" She was so engrossed in finishing the last couple of bites that it was a few minutes before she noticed Craig looking at her funny.

She grinned and then felt pizza grease run down her chin. Before she could bend over and pick up a napkin, Craig moved the box and quickly pulled her to him. They could never eat pizza after that without smiling at each other.

Jenna tried to speak but she had no words. What do you say to your teenage daughter that you just caught having sex? Was there anything more mortifying? Would she ever get that image out of her head?

Abby covered herself with the blanket that was lying on the couch.

"I'm really sorry, Mom. I don't know what else to say." She stuck her thumb in her mouth and chewed on the nail nervously.

Jenna closed her eyes and took a deep breath and then looked at her daughter.

"I don't know what to say either. Just tell me you used protection."

When Abby was silent, Jenna stared wide-eyed at her daughter. In a panic she yelled, "You didn't use protection?!"

Abby looked down and mumbled, "We didn't need to."

"What do you mean you didn't need to? Did you not listen to any of our conversations? You want to get pregnant or get an STD?"

Jenna was so stunned that it took a moment for Abby's words to sink in.

"Please tell me you're not pregnant." She looked at Abby, willing those words to be true. "Oh, Abby, please tell me you're not pregnant!"

"I can't!" Abby cried and hung her head shamefully.

Jenna doubled over in pain. Would this nightmare never end? It was inconceivable that her daughter was pregnant. This had to be a joke. She couldn't comprehend it, and the shock left her speechless.

"Mom, it's been so ... so awful with dad gone. Isaac has been wonderful, and he's been there when I needed him. We bought a pregnancy test this morning from the drug store and it was positive."

When Jenna sat there dumbfounded and mute, Abby kept talking. "We love each other. Isaac has been so sweet, and I don't know what I would have done without him."

Jenna looked at her daughter, her daughter who was 16 and still looked like a child. What did she know about love? She still fussed when her mom didn't buy her favorite cereal or cried when Jenna wouldn't let her go to parties. Jenna chastised herself for not knowing that her child was having sex. She should have known. Was she so much into her own grief that she didn't see the signs? Of course, Isaac took advantage of Abby's vulnerability. She told her daughter that. "Honey, can't you see that Isaac used you?"

Abby looked mortified. "It's not like that! He loves me and I love him."

Jenna shook her head and tried to stay calm. "Will he still love you when he can't go to college because he has a wife and baby?"

"I didn't say we were getting married or keeping the baby."

Jenna narrowed her eyes at her daughter and in disbelief said, "Excuse me?"

"We have options. If I am really pregnant, it's not too late for an abortion or I can have the baby and give it to someone who wants to adopt it. Either way, Isaac and I are way too young to get married and raise a baby together."

Rolling her eyes toward the bedroom, Jenna said, "You're way too young to be doing that too." Jenna stood up and began to pace in front of the couch. "Can you really see yourself killing an innocent baby?"

"It's not like that. It's not even formed yet."

"It's further along than you realize. In no time the doctors will be able to detect a heartbeat."

"I haven't decided anyway," Abby said with a stubborn look.

Jenna began rubbing her temples, trying to ease the pounding in her head. What would Craig say? What would Craig do? Taking a deep breath, Jenna tried to get through to her daughter. "This is so much more complicated than you realize!" Sitting back down on the couch, she placed her hand on her daughter's thigh. "I don't want you to live with regrets the rest of your life, Abby. Please think about this. There's a consequence to any decision you make... just make sure it's the consequence you can live with."

Abby nodded, big fat tears rolling down her cheeks. Jenna was reminded of the day she took a four-year-old Abby to the doctor to get her cast removed after she had fallen off the swing set and broke her leg. Jenna tried to explain to her that they used a saw to remove the cast and that it would be very loud, but it wouldn't touch her leg and wouldn't hurt her. She would never forget how Abby held her head high, determined not to cry, even a little bit, but one big fat tear fell unbidden down her cheek. The doctor and nurse were amazed.

Abby looked down and picked at her nails. "I'm so sorry. We didn't mean for it to happen, it...it just did. Isaac did use protection that first time."

Jenna couldn't help it. Her heart went out to her daughter, and she vowed she would do anything and everything to help her in any way she could.

"It happens sometimes, Abby. I just hate that it happened to you, but we'll deal with it. That's all we can do." She paused and then took her hand. "Please think long and hard about this. We'll get through it together, I promise."

Abby suddenly jumped up and fell into her mother's arms. "Thank you, Mom! I've been so scared." Taking a tissue from the coffee table, she blew her nose. "Daddy would be so mad at me. Would he ever forgive me?"

Jenna pulled Abby close. "Of course he would forgive you." Taking Abby's long dark hair that was just like her own, she smoothed it down her back. "He would be extremely upset and probably kick Isaac's butt though."

Jenna held her for a long time, wondering what in the world she was going to do now.

Chapter 6

Ben raised his bed up so he could watch the morning news. The world was passing him by while he was stuck in the hospital. Climate change was causing havoc and politics were front and center with a new president at the helm. Ben changed the channels, but the same story was on all three of the major news networks, so he turned it off, not caring if the new president could change the United States in the few short weeks he had been in office. He did know one thing; one side would be for it, one side against it.

Ben was feeling better every day, so he knew it wouldn't be too much longer before he was released. The threat of rejection had passed, and he was getting stronger. A sweet lady named Nora came in with a breakfast tray and placed it on the table next to his bed.

"Thank you, Nora."

"You're welcome, Ben. You sure are looking better."

Ben smiled. "Thank you, I feel a lot better." Before Nora could leave, Nancy walked in carrying fast food bags, which she tried to hide.

"Good morning, Benji." She nodded at Nora as she left the room and then pulled out a small bag from McDonald's, whispering, "I brought you an egg McMuffin" like she was breaking the law or something.

"I know how you love them, and I figured you might be getting tired of hospital food." She placed it next to his breakfast tray and then busied herself with preparing his food. She opened his carton of juice and took the lid off his coffee.

Ben noticed that she was wearing one of her many velour tracksuits, her favorite winter attire. Today's ensemble was a bright wine color. Her short blonde hair was perfectly styled, not a hair out of place. "Thanks, Mom, I am getting a little tired of it. It's not horrible but it's not the best either." Ben unwrapped the sandwich and took a bite, savoring the combination of egg, cheese, and ham on the warm muffin. His appetite was getting stronger. Hopefully he would begin gaining back some of the weight he had lost over the last year. His coloring was much better and his scar, while still ugly and red, was healing nicely.

Nancy pulled some greeting cards out of her satchel and placed them in front of Ben. "Here are some get-well cards from church and your work. Brittany said to tell you that they miss you and can't wait until you come back." Nancy grinned. "She's called me several times. I think she might just have a tiny crush on you."

Ben rolled his eyes. "Brittany is married. Happily so."

Nancy looked disappointed. "Really? Well, anyway, I've been getting your room ready. There's not a spot of dust anywhere and everything has been disinfected."

Ben wasn't surprised. His mother had always been a meticulous housekeeper. Most of the furniture had been around a long time, but it was in perfect shape.

Ben finished his muffin and wiped his mouth with a napkin. After taking a sip of coffee, he said, "Thanks, Mom, I really appreciate you letting me stay there temporarily." Ben wanted to make sure his mom knew it was not forever and didn't want her to get her hopes up.

"You can stay there forever if you want to. I'm just so excited I could bust! Having you home again will be like old times. We can watch television and I'll cook all your favorite meals until we've fattened you up. I've been getting all kinds of new recipes on Facebook, but I promise I won't cook food that's bad for you. I was at the grocery store yesterday and guess what I saw? Plain salt. Why, I've been buying iodized salt for as long as I can remember. I was afraid to buy the plain stuff."

Nancy stopped talking when her phone dinged in her pocketbook. She fished it out and looked at it and then placed it back in her bag. "That's Sarah again. She keeps asking about you. I've tried to give her updates when I can. I hope that's okay."

Ben noticed she didn't seem too happy about it. "That's fine, but I hope she doesn't come here. I really don't want to see her."

"I know. I told her that you can't really have visitors, which isn't a complete lie. They really do discourage anyone from coming, you know—germs and all." Nancy busied herself cleaning up Ben's breakfast tray and threw the McDonald's bag and wrapper away.

"I brought your iPad and your briefcase. Don't do too much and get tired." She took them out of her bag and placed them on the table in front of him. "Brittany mailed some stuff and I put that in your briefcase. She said it's nothing urgent, just some things you can look at when you feel like it."

When Nancy finally sat down and pulled her yarn and needle out, Ben rifled through his briefcase. Brittany had enclosed some specifications of mechanical and lighting aspects of a building in downtown Charlotte the firm was working on along with some contracts to sign. Once he was done, Ben laid back, closing his eyes. He hadn't done much, but he felt as if he had run a marathon. He would have to rest before they came to help him with his shower.

"Are you okay, Benji?" He could hear the concern in his mother's voice.

Ben didn't open his eyes. "I'm fine, Mom. Just need to rest a little bit."

"I'll get the nurse or even the doctor if you need me to. Just say the word."

"No, I'm good." Ben eventually fell asleep to the comfortable chatter of his mother droning on and on about everything and nothing.

Chapter 7

"She what?!" If it wasn't so serious, Jenna could have laughed at the surprised expression on her best friend's face. "You can't be serious!" Rachel's mouth was wide open in surprise.

"Do you think I would joke about something like that? Let me assure you, this is very real and she's definitely pregnant," Jenna said. "I took her to my gynecologist, and he confirmed it. She's about six weeks along."

Jenna and Rachel were having their usual Friday night get-together, which consisted of a movie, take-out, and a bottle of Diet Coke. Rachel would end up spending the night and they would go Christmas shopping at the outlet stores the next day.

"Good grief. What is she going to do?" Rachel opened her container of honey chicken and rice and stirred the food with a plastic fork.

"Abby has decided not to have an abortion." Jenna took a sip of her soda and then shook her head. "I'm glad she's not having an abortion, but I have no idea what's going to happen after that."

Rachel looked at Jenna in understanding, taking her hand and patting it. "I'm so sorry, sweetie. What about school? She certainly can't walk around school pregnant."

"Once she begins to show, the school will put her on homebound. That's all we can do at this point. One day at a time." Jenna looked up. "Help me, Jesus."

Maybe if Jenna told herself this enough, she would finally begin to believe it. Finally telling someone that her daughter was pregnant had actually been a relief. Without Craig, Jenna felt a huge void and would find herself close to full-blown panic attacks trying to deal with it all on her own.

"How in the world have you coped with this all by yourself? I can't believe you didn't tell me." Rachel looked offended.

Jenna poured more soda in their glasses and then took a sip. "To be honest, it's been horrible. I wanted to tell you, but I've been in shock myself."

"I knew you were having a hard time, but I thought it was all because of losing Craig. I had no idea something else was going on." Rachel's eyes suddenly widened. "Have you told your mom?"

Jenna made a funny face. "Good grief, no! I'm waiting until the last possible moment." Just imagining the disappointed look on her mother's face was enough to give Jenna palpitations. Jenna and Abby planned on telling the family once the holidays were over. They decided to let them at least have some peace until then. She didn't even know if Isaac's family was aware of the situation. He was still afraid to show his face, but Jenna knew that he and Abby were still talking. Abby said that he was behind her one hundred percent, whatever that meant.

Chip, who had been nestled between them, jumped up when he heard a noise. Jenna and Rachel both looked up and saw Abby walk into the living room looking sheepish. She sat down in the chair.

"I guess Mom told you the big, terrible news."

Rachel, who never held back her feelings or minced words, raised her eyebrows and said, "Yes she did, young lady, and I have to say I'm really disappointed in you."

Abby closed her eyes and hung her head. Rachel looked at Jenna and rolled her eyes, well aware of Abby's tendencies towards the dramatic. "Look at me, Abby."

Abby looked up at Rachel, surprised at her tone. "Yes, I'm disappointed, but you're not the first young girl to get knocked up. Matter of fact, I got knocked up when I was in high school."

Jenna and Abby both gasped.

"Yes, it's true." Rachel waved her hands. "I apologize for not telling you before, Jenna, but it's not something you want to advertise." She took a deep breath. "I was 15 years old when I got pregnant. I let myself be talked into skipping school with an older boy I thought was the greatest thing since sliced bread. He was handsome and popular and a real jerk. He took advantage of me and... well, we had sex before I even knew what happened. For months I ignored it until I couldn't ignore it anymore. My parents found out and sent me to live with my aunt in South Carolina until I had the baby."

Rachel paused and closed her eyes. "I only saw him once, and he was absolutely beautiful. He had a head full of black hair and the cutest little dimple on his chin."

They were all quiet, Jenna and Abby shocked into silence and Rachel remembering her heartbreak like it had just happened. She sniffed and wiped a tear from her eye.

"So, I know what you're going through, Abby. I can be here for both of you if you need me."

Abby and Jenna both jumped up and hugged Rachel, wiping their noses with their sleeves.

Once they were all spent with their crying and hugging, Rachel said, "It's something you never forget and you carry it with you always, wondering what if. I've played that game a million times. Now here I am, 40 years old with no husband and no children and new boobs. Life sure is full of surprises."

Jenna looked at her dear friend and her heart broke. "Do you know anything about him? Where he is or how he's doing?"

Rachel shook her head. "No. I gave my permission for him to contact me if he wanted to, but he never has. He could be in South Carolina, but I don't know. He's 27 years old now. I could be a grandmother."

"Wouldn't that be something, though, if he did contact you?" Jenna asked.

"I think about it all the time. Sometimes he's angry. Sometimes he's happy that he's found me. Sometimes I even imagine that he's forgiven me and wants to be a part of my life." Realizing that she spoke her private thoughts out loud, Rachel looked embarrassed.

They both looked at Abby, who was sitting in the chair lost in thought. They knew that she was finally realizing the full ramifications of her pregnancy. Whatever decisions she made would be hard ones. Whatever decisions she made would also have lasting consequences. There were no easy answers.

Abby finally looked up and asked Rachel, "Do you regret giving him away?"

Rachel looked knowingly at Abby.

"Sometimes I do and sometimes I don't," she said. "In a perfect world, yes, I would have loved to have been able to keep him and raise him, but it wasn't a perfect world, Abby. My parents were embarrassed and ashamed of me. Bringing him home to live with them wasn't even an option. His father wasn't in the picture. I did tell him, eventually, but he said it was my problem and to deal with it. So, without any kind of support, I felt I didn't have a say, and my parents made the choice for me."

Rachel stopped talking and then placed her hand on her lips. "But sometimes I think that I made a mistake. I should have walked through fire to keep my child with me. He was mine and he was my responsibility, and nobody would love him like me.

"Look, I wish I could give you an easy answer, sweetie, but there are none. But at least you have a mom who is there for you in whatever decision you make."

Jenna nodded and smiled.

Abby took a bite of one of the egg rolls on the coffee table and then looked thoughtful. "It almost doesn't even seem real yet. At first, Isaac was okay, but then he acted like he wanted me to have an abortion, but I told him I can't do that. I googled pictures of what the baby looks like and what happens in an abortion. I told him and it freaked him out too."

Jenna and Rachel looked at each other but didn't say anything.

"Sometimes I pretend that it's not real and that I'm really not pregnant, but I know I can't do that anymore. Isaac and I need to decide what we need to do." Abby stood up. "I think I'm going to call him right now."

Jenna and Rachel watched Abby walk out of the living room and to her bedroom.

Jenna said, "Maybe she's finally getting it."

She turned and looked at her friend in amazement. "I can't believe you never told me this."

Rachel took a deep breath. "It's hard, Jenna. Talking about it just brings up so much hurt and I can't stand it. It's easier to try and forget." She took Jenna's hand, "So what do you think? Are you willing to help raise this baby or would you rather it be adopted?"

Jenna grimaced. "I don't know, Rachel. If Craig were here, I know we would gladly take the baby and help all we could. I just don't know if I could do it on my own." She shook her head. "Raising Abby was so hard. She was colicky and I almost went crazy. I would have if Craig hadn't been there."

Rachel nodded. "I know, but could you let the baby go, knowing you might never see it again? What if it's a boy and he looked like Craig?"

Big, fat tears began falling down Jenna's face. Rachel grabbed some tissues from the coffee table, giving them to Jenna but keeping one for herself. "I just don't want you to have regrets, sweetie. I know all about regrets. I've lived with them all my life. You and Abby won't be by yourselves because you will definitely have my support too."

Jenna wiped her eyes and smiled. "You know that means the world to me and you're right, somehow we've got to keep this baby. Craig would be so disappointed in me if we didn't."

Chapter 8

Ben was finally able to leave the hospital. His heart transplant had been a success and so far, his body had decided to keep the new heart instead of rejecting it. He was lying in his childhood bedroom studying the teenage décor that his mother couldn't bring herself to get rid of. Ben was surprised to find out that she couldn't bear to throw away anything, even his old Kurt Cobain posters. He could see his faded high school swim medals stapled haphazardly to a cork board and a bunch of cross-country trophies lined up on the wall shelf. There was a picture of Ben and his dad on the dresser, their arms around each other. Ben had always loved that picture. It was the last photo taken of them together before he died.

All in all, he felt pretty good. The extreme fatigue that plagued him before seemed to be getting better. He still had some pain, which doctors said was normal after having your whole chest cavity opened up. Six months of recovery seemed like a long time, but Ben was thankful that at least he was finally on that road. Hopefully in less than six weeks he would be able to go back to work depending on how his sternum had healed. He didn't like the fact that he would be on meds for the rest of his life and that he would be medically supervised, but it was better than the alternative.

Thinking back to that day he was ready to give up everything gave him chills. He now wanted to live his life and live it to the absolute fullest.

God gave him another chance, which happened to be at the expense of someone else, which was hard to bear, but he promised that he wouldn't waste a minute of his life and he would try and honor that person every single day. He couldn't help but wonder who that person might be. Was it a man, a woman, or a child? To know he had that person's heart in his own body was mind boggling. He wanted to know everything about him or her. When the time was right, he planned on contacting that family. Wouldn't they want to know about him as well?

He carefully got out of bed and grabbed his robe and headed for the bathroom. He was very thankful that he had his mom to help him with his recovery, but he was ready to go home. Now that he was given the okay to drive, he felt it was time, but the look on his mother's face every time he mentioned it stopped him in his tracks. Sad look or not, today he was going to tell her that he was going home.

After he had showered and dressed, he walked into the kitchen just as his mother was setting the breakfast table. "Perfect timing, what do you want to drink, Benji?"

Ben mumbled, "Milk, please."

"I made your favorite, blueberry pancakes and chicken sausage. How about we do a little Christmas shopping today? I also need to go by the post office and mail your sister's package. Laura probably won't like it, she never does, but how am I supposed to know what she likes when she never comes around? Have you thought anymore about what you want for Christmas? I was thinking about getting you a..."

"Mom, could you stop for just a minute?"

Nancy's eyes widened. "I was just..."

"I know. I know. I just need to talk to you about something, something important." Ben noticed his mom biting her lip, anticipating what he was about to say and trying to stop him with all her might. He knew she had enjoyed having him around the house again. She loved cooking for him and taking care of him, which he appreciated, but he had to go home before she became too dependent on his company.

"We don't have to go shopping. We can just stay around here and watch television or something. There's a great movie on this afternoon, you know, your favorite, um, what's it called?"

"Mom, I'm going to move back to my place today." There, he said it. And now it begins ...

"Heavens, son, there's no sense in you moving back home. Why, this old house is big enough for 10 people. You don't have to cook or clean or even wash your clothes. I promise I won't..."

Interrupting her once again, he said, "Mom, you can never know how much I appreciate all you've done for me, but I need to be in my own place. I love you but... aw, now please don't cry." Nancy's eyes were filling with tears as if on cue. He hated to hurt her feelings, but sometimes it felt as if she treated him like a husband instead of her son.

"What about your friend, Larry Ledbetter?" Ben said. You don't even spend time with him anymore."

"Larry? I don't have to spend time with him; he's just a friend, nothing more." She narrowed her eyes for emphasis. "Besides, I can't think about him when my son needs me." Now she looked extremely offended.

"I just don't want to interfere with your life. You've done your job and I'm recovering wonderfully. Unfortunately, the bills are piling up and I need to get to work."

"You can't go to work yet!"

"I can work at home at first. I'll start off slow and build myself up until I can eventually go to the office full time."

"I still don't see why you can't do that here."

"Please try and understand, Mom."

Nancy turned from the kitchen table and began cleaning up the mess on the stove. Once she finished, she began washing the dishes. In frustration, Ben said, "Aren't you going to eat?"

Without even turning around, she said, "I'm not hungry."

Ben groaned and began stuffing a sausage into his mouth. He knew he had to stand his ground, or he would be there for life. She would get over it... eventually. Once he finished, he tried to wash his plate, but his mother only shooed him out of the kitchen.

He decided that it was now or never, so he grabbed some of his things and headed towards the front door.

His mom was there in a flash, dish towel thrown across her shoulder. "You're leaving now?"

"Yeah, I wanted to see if everything was okay. I'll come back this evening for the rest of my things. How about I take you to Olive Garden tonight for dinner? My treat."

Sighing dramatically, she said, "I guess that would be okay." Nancy loved Olive Garden and never turned down an invitation to eat there.

Kissing her on the cheek, Ben smiled, "Great. I'll see you in a bit. Love you, Mom." He didn't wait for a response but was out the door and headed for freedom.

Ben's apartment was silent and cold. He turned the heat up and turned the television on. Everything was as dreary as it was the last time he was there. After he and Sarah separated, he leased the apartment mostly because of its location. It was close to the interstate and made for an easy commute to Charlotte. Once he moved in, he had no interest or energy to make it into any kind of home. It had just the bare necessities and nothing more. He hadn't even lived there long enough to really call it home.

Tired from the morning exertion, he sat down on the secondhand couch his mom had given him and began surfing channels. He could watch anything he wanted. When watching TV at his mom's house, she would sit there with her needle and yarn exclaiming, "You want to watch that? You know such-in-such is on, don't you? It's a really good show." Her hints were never subtle. Even when Ben was interested in something, his mom would talk the entire time. When she was on her iPad it was worse. All of her friends were on Facebook now, and Nancy was afraid she would miss something if she didn't look at it at least 10 times a day. She liked to watch videos, and the volume would be so loud that the neighbors next door heard it too.

Ben leaned his head back and closed his eyes. He felt relaxed and began to drift off to sleep. When he woke with a start, he looked at the clock on the wall and realized he had been asleep for at least an hour. Ben remembered he had been having a dream and it was so real. A beautiful woman with long dark hair had been running ahead of him through some kind of park. He kept trying to catch her, but every time he was close, she would slip away again. All of a sudden, she had grabbed him from behind and whirled him around. Her hands were on his chest, and they slowly inched their way up until she had them locked around his neck. She stepped closer and closer until she was flush against him, feeling the part of him that wanted her desperately. She smiled knowingly, pulling his lips towards hers, but then the dream ended.

Ben looked down at his pants and muttered, "Well, at least that part still works."

He scratched his head and thought about the woman in his dream. He was pretty sure he had never seen her before. She had the bluest eyes and beautiful long dark hair that he knew was silky to the touch, even though he hadn't touched it. Shaking his head and releasing a pent-up breath, Ben began rubbing his eyes. He didn't know who she was, but he knew for certain that he would never forget her.

His phone began vibrating, alerting him to an incoming text. When he saw Sarah's name pop up, he was surprised. He knew that his mom had continued to update Sarah on his condition after the surgery, but he still had no desire to talk to her at all. His curiosity got the better of him though, so he opened the text and read, *Talked to your mom. Glad you're doing better! Can I come over this evening? I have something I need to talk to you about.* He really wanted to text her back and say, *No thanks. I have nothing to say to you,* but he couldn't. Instead, he sent, *Having dinner with Mom so tonight is not a good time.* She responded promptly with, *I can come now. I'll bring lunch!*

Ben gritted his teeth, irritated. That was one thing that really drove him crazy about Sarah. She never took no for an answer, and everything always had to be her way. At first it had been endearing, but now he found it annoying. He really had no excuse so out of frustration he responded, K, knowing that she hated short, unemotional responses. She always complained he never showed any personality in his texts or emails. She had exclamation points after every sentence along with emojis cataloging her every mood.

Ben got out his laptop and began checking his emails from work. Before he knew it, the doorbell was ringing. Taking his time, he finally answered the door to find a smiling Sarah standing on his threshold holding a bag of Chinese take-out.

"Oh my goodness, Ben, look at you. I can't believe this!"

Ben stepped aside, letting her enter his apartment. She put the food on the kitchen counter and placed her hands on her hips.

"I've prayed and prayed that you would make it through the transplant surgery okay and now here you are." She tried to brighten her smile, but she was having a hard time of it.

Ben wondered if she was taking credit for his recovery, which was definitely like her. Ben also knew he didn't look so good. He had lost a ton of weight and his skin was pale. Sarah would be freaked out by the huge, long ugly scar on his chest too. The way he looked at it, if he didn't have that scar, he would be dead.

"Is there anything I can do? I know this is your first day back at your apartment. I can go to the market for you. Let's make a list and I'll go this afternoon." Sarah began rummaging through her purse for pen and paper.

Ben hated that he had to lean against the counter for support because he didn't want to show any weakness. "No, Sarah. I don't need anything. Why are you here?" He had been fine before Sarah showed up but now felt weak and clammy.

Looking deflated, she began biting her lip. "I do need to talk to you about something, but let's eat first, okay? I brought soup and egg rolls and your favorite, veggie lo mien." She groped inside the bags until she brought all of the contents out and set them on the counter. "Looks like we need to fatten you up a bit."

"Sarah, stop. Just tell me what's on your mind." He hated to be so blunt, but he really couldn't handle this whole situation. Once, Ben thought she was the sweetest, kindest person he ever knew, but now he understood that she wasn't any of those things. How could you leave someone who you professed to love when they needed you the most? She failed the most important test of a relationship. She was only sweet and kind when it suited her.

Looking completely baffled, Sarah whispered, "I was only trying to help." The quivering lip, which once looked so endearing, now only looked fake and irksome.

Ben looked at her, trying to remain calm, not even bothering to respond. Sarah took a deep breath, looked down at the floor and said, "I just wanted you to know that... that I'm moving on with my life." She paused, waiting for Ben to say something, but he kept silent, so she finally looked up. "I've met someone. We're engaged. I... I just felt that I needed to tell you before you heard it from someone else."

Sarah actually had the gall to look at him with pity in her eyes, which irritated him even more.

"Fine, you told me. I really have some work to do."

Exasperated, Sarah said, "Is that all you have to say?"

"What do you want me to say, Sarah?"

Sarah gaped at him in frustration. "Maybe, 'Congratulations?' 'Good luck?' Or maybe, 'Are you sure this is what you want to do?' I don't know, Ben, maybe something that tells me you have some kind of emotion!"

Ben shrugged. "You want emotion? I really don't know what you expect me to say, Sarah." Ben rubbed the area between his eyebrows and then waved his hand. "Go. Get married. I don't care what you do; it makes no difference to me."

In complete shock, Sarah gasped, her eyes wide and holding her hand to her mouth for extra dramatic effect. He was so immune to her antics that he just rolled his eyes.

Sarah dropped her hands in a huff and walked to the counter to grab her purse and stomped to the door mumbling, "I was only trying to help."

Before she exited, she paused as if she had one last thing to say, but evidently thought better of it and left. Ben promptly took all the bags containing the food and dumped them in the trash, muttering, "And I hate veggie lo mien, by the way. That was *your* favorite."

Chapter 9

The holidays were over and now Jenna and Abby had the task of telling the family about Abby's pregnancy. She wished more than anything that she didn't have to tell them, but keeping it a secret was beginning to stress her.

Jenna and Abby had already talked to Isaac's parents about Abby keeping the baby. Isaac's parents assured everyone that they would help emotionally and financially. Jenna had her concerns, but everyone assured her they were all on board. Abby would finish high school and Isaac would go to the University of North Carolina at Chapel Hill as he had intended. It was his parents' alma mater, and it was their hope that he would follow in their footsteps and become a lawyer too.

Abby still had no idea what she wanted to do, but she didn't want to give her baby away and Jenna didn't want her to, either.

Jenna closed her eyes and wished for the thousandth time that Craig hadn't died. Knowing Craig, he would probably have already adjusted to the idea of being a grandfather and would be looking forward to it. He always made the best of every situation. One time, when Abby was about three or four, he found Jenna crying in the bathroom. Financially, things were pretty tough. Teacher salaries were certainly not the best and they had over-extended themselves. Jenna didn't have enough to pay the house payment and her worse fear was losing it after they had worked so hard to buy it.

Craig took her in his arms and before she knew it, she was laughing and wondering why she had been upset in the first place. He always made her feel better. With him, nothing was impossible. Somehow, he found the money to pay all the bills that month, and he also started a side job with a couple of other coaches painting houses. Times weren't always easy, but with Craig, you didn't worry so much.

Jenna looked at her watch and realized it was almost time for everyone to come over. She had invited her mom, Craig's parents, and Isaac's parents to come to the house for coffee and cake. Of course, Abby was there, and Rachel was coming for moral support. She walked into the kitchen to check on the coffee cake. Chip followed and wove himself in and around her legs as she stood, enjoying the aroma of cinnamon. Opening the oven, she pulled out the cake and set it on the top of the stove to let it cool.

"Wow that smells good!" Rachel came in the kitchen door and hung her pocketbook on the wall hook. "At least everyone will enjoy the cake before you spring the good news on them, you follow? Cluck cluck." She walked to the stove and took a big whiff. "You may need to get some barf bags ready in case anyone throws it back up."

Jenna stuck her tongue out. "I think I may need a barf bag right now. Can you get some paper plates and cups out of the pantry for me and put them on the dining room table?" As they both busied themselves around the kitchen, the doorbell rang. "Okay, here goes. Wish me luck."

Rachel mumbled something about needing more than luck, causing Jenna to give her a dirty look.

Elizabeth was the first to show up. "What in the world is going on?" She stood right in front of the door holding her pocketbook in front of her chest and wouldn't budge until Jenna finally begged her to come in and sit down.

"Everyone should be here any minute, and then we'll explain everything." Jenna brought a hot cup of black coffee and handed it to Elizabeth. She then watched Abby and Isaac slowly walk in the living room, sitting down in one of the dining room chairs Jenna had placed earlier.

Sitting with her pocketbook on her lap, Jenna's mother clucked softly and then placed the cup on the coffee table in front of the couch. "It's something really bad, isn't it?" She looked at Abby and Isaac suspiciously.

Jenna shook her head. "Please don't get worked up. It's not the end of the world, I promise." Before Elizabeth could respond, Bill, Lynn, and Isaac's parents were coming through the front door.

"Come on in." Jenna took their coats and handed them to Rachel who was standing close by. "Renee and Phillip are Isaac's parents. This is Elizabeth Johnston, my mother. Bill and Lynn are Craig's parents. Have a seat everyone."

Jenna looked at Rachel for support because at any moment she felt as if her legs would give out. Rachel gave her a goofy look and a *thumbs up* gesture that almost made Jenna laugh. She knew if she did laugh that she probably wouldn't be able to stop.

"Abby has some news she wants to share with you. Would y'all like some coffee? I made a coffee cake too... just got it out of the oven."

Elizabeth shook her head. "I can't eat a bite until you tell me what's going on. My stomach is a topsy-turvy mess."

Jenna took a deep breath and then looked at Abby. Abby shook her head. Jenna didn't blame her. She wished she could shake her own head. "Renee and Phillip already know the big news, but they wanted to be here for moral support." Jenna cleared her throat. "Abby and Isaac are expecting a baby at the end of July."

A loud gasp exploded from Elizabeth as she stood up. Fanning her face and clucking like a hen laying a double-yolk egg, she looked directly at Isaac. "But...but you're black!"

Rachel had a straight face, but Jenna knew her well enough to know she was laughing inside. Lynn kept repeating, "Oh my, oh my, oh my," while rocking back and forth. Bill sat forward, placing his hands on his thighs and kept clearing his throat like he had something stuck in it.

Jenna wondered how long it would take for her mother to bring up the racial difference and obviously it wasn't long at all. Jenna hung her head and said a quick prayer for guidance. "I think we all know that, Mama." She looked at Isaac and then his parents with an apologetic look. All three looked uncomfortable.

Abby's lower lip was puckered out, and Jenna knew that any minute she would start crying. "I know it's a shocker, but it's not the end of the world." She finally sat down on one of the dining room chairs for fear of falling down. "Once you all get used to the idea, you'll realize that, in some ways, it's a blessing." Trying to ignore the loud gasp from her mom, Jenna said, "Abby is going to keep the baby, and we'll all raise it together. He or she will be loved and have everything they will ever need. I know if Craig..." Jenna almost choked on her words but continued, "I know if Craig were here, he would be happy and make the best of the situation, and I hope you all will too."

Bill shook his head. "Well, it ain't the first baby to come before anyone was ready, and it won't be the last." He turned and looked at his wife. "Right, Lynn?"

Lynn turned several shades of red and shook her head quickly. "No, I reckon not." She nodded and said, "And you're right, Jenna. Craig would make the best of the situation and I know he would love this little baby."

Jenna smiled through her tears and got up to hug Lynn. "Thank you, that means a lot." She looked at her mother who still sat clutching her purse as if it was a lifeline. "Are you okay, Mama?"

Elizabeth took a deep breath. "Have you thought of the ramifications of having an interracial child? Have you all thought of what this child will go through?"

Phillip, Isaac's father, finally spoke up. "And what's that supposed to mean?"

Not one to back down an inch, Elizabeth looked him straight in the eye. "I mean, this child will not fit in with the whites or blacks, you follow?"

Phillip looked visibly shaken, but Renee patted his arm and spoke calmly. "I think that in this day and age, things are a little bit different than they used to be, Mrs. Johnston. I, for one, will love this baby no matter what its skin color is."

Jenna could tell that Isaac wanted to speak but couldn't quite get the words out. "Is there something you want to say, Isaac?"

Isaac nodded. "Yes, Mrs. Rogers, I just wanted to say that I know it's a shock for everyone." He looked at Abby. "Abby and I are very sorry for all the trouble we've caused. We hope that with everyone's love and support, we can make sure this baby is happy and taken care of." Isaac sat down and Abby grabbed his arm and squeezed.

Jenna couldn't help but be impressed with Isaac. She knew that had to be the hardest speech he'd probably ever made.

"Thank you, Isaac. I'm sure my mother will eventually realize that we're all just trying to do the best we can." She looked at her mother questionably. "Right, Mama?"

Elizabeth slowly sat down still clutching her purse. She looked at Abby. "Young lady, I just want you to know that this is the last thing I expected and I'm not going to lie; I am disappointed. I wish this could have waited until the appropriate time, when you're married of course, but you're not, and there's nothing we can do but make the best of it. I will be here for you and your mother just as I always am."

Abby, looking sheepish, muttered, "Thank you, Nana."

Elizabeth nodded. "Okay, I'm ready for cake now."

After everyone had left, Jenna was cleaning up the kitchen and Rachel was straightening up the living room. They were both quiet until Jenna heard Rachel giggle. Wondering what in the world she was giggling about, she put the dish towel over her shoulder and went to investigate only to find Rachel falling back on the couch, her giggles turning into laughter.

"What is so funny?"

Rachel was laughing so hard, tears were streaming down her face. "Your mother!"

Jenna smirked. "Yeah, she's a real hoot. And in case you don't recognize it, that's sarcasm."

"I wish you could have seen the look on your face when your mom looked at Isaac and said, 'But you're black!'" Rachel doubled over she was laughing so hard.

Jenna wondered if Rachel was losing it, and then a small giggle escaped her own mouth. Before she knew it, she was laughing right alongside her best friend.

Later, Jenna sat in silence in the darkened living room thinking about all that had happened earlier. The only sound was purring. Chip was curled up next to Jenna on the sofa.

Jenna still couldn't believe it. Soon they would have a sweet little baby and she would continue to be a part of its life. Maybe it would be a boy. Craig would have been so happy. It was so unfair that he would never know his own grandchild.

Chip began stretching his legs and then licked his paws. Absently, Jenna began stroking his fur. What if the whole situation became too much for both Abby and Isaac? What if they changed their minds? Jenna vowed that she would never let that happen. She would not lose this baby. He or she would always know love, and even though Craig was gone, the baby would always know who he was. She would make sure of it.

Jenna shook her head and wondered how things had turned around so quickly. Finding out that Abby was pregnant had devastated her and now... well, now there was so much hope. This precious baby was everything. She picked up Chip and cuddled him close.

"Just wait, Chip, soon there will be a baby in the house. What do you think of that?" Chip meowed and Jenna laughed.

Chapter 10

Ben sat at his desk at work analyzing the design of a new building project that his firm was working on. It felt so good to be back at work, being productive and contributing to society. At first, his co-workers acted like he would keel over at any time. Getting aggravated, he put his hands over his heart as if he was having a heart attack scaring everyone to death at one of their meetings. He looked up with one eye at all the shocked faces and then started laughing. "Look people; I had a heart transplant but I'm good to go now. Stop treating me like I've got one foot in the grave."

Pretty soon it became a big joke, and they all began grabbing their chests at every opportune moment when they didn't want to do something. Ben's mother didn't see the joke at all. If he didn't call her at least twice a day, she would be calling him. It was embarrassing having your mother call you at work.

"Mr. Thompson, your mother is on line two."

Oh crap! She had called earlier on his cell while he was in a meeting, and he forgot to call back.

"Hey, Mom, sorry I forgot to call. I'm fine; it's just been a busy morning."

"You know how I worry. I just can't be satisfied until I hear your voice."

Don't I know it, Ben thought. "It's okay."

"I'm fixing a chicken casserole for dinner tonight. Why don't you come over and eat? NCIS comes on tonight."

Ben loved his mother dearly, but sometimes he felt so smothered. "I'm sorry, I can't. I have to get groceries. I'm out of everything, including milk."

"Just give me a list and I'll get everything for you. I'm headed out to the store anyway."

Ben took an exasperating breath. "I appreciate it, but I need to go myself. I'm going to the supercenter to get some stuff for the apartment too. It's time to make it more like a home."

"I still don't know why you can't just move back here. We could have so much fun, and you wouldn't have to lift a finger."

"Mom, please, let's not get into that again. I need to have my own space. Look, I need to get back to work. I promise I'll be over Sunday."

"Will you at least go to church with me, Benji? Please?" Her church had a new pastor that she was excited about, and she had been aggravating him to go. "I know you'll love it! There are lots of young people."

It had been a long time since Ben had gone to church. He sighed and rubbed the bridge of his nose with his finger and thumb. Knowing that his mother was relentless and wouldn't give up, Ben gave in. "Okay, okay. I'll go."

"Wonderful! I'll save you some leftovers and bring them by your apartment tomorrow. I love you and I'll talk to you this evening."

Ben hung up shaking his head. He had given his mother a key to his apartment and now regretted it. She would go by and "tidy up" or leave leftovers in his fridge all the time. He was going to have to find something for her to do. She had too much energy to just sit around all day. She needed a life. Maybe then she wouldn't be in his business all the time. Ben's secretary, Brittany, said he had the patience of a saint. But Ben knew that his mother was there for him when nobody else was. He wouldn't hurt her for the world.

As Ben was getting ready for church Sunday morning, he already regretted telling his mother that he would go with her. His life was slowly getting back to normal. He looked forward to the weekends to relax and do whatever he wanted. He was becoming addicted to Netflix. Sunday was movie day and he loved being lazy. Some Sundays he didn't even take a shower.

His mother may get mad, but he was just going to have to tell her no from now on. She would get over it. Church just wasn't his thing.

Nancy was waiting at the front door as Ben pulled in the driveway. She pulled the door shut and locked it with her key. Her smile was wide as she walked to the car.

"I'm so glad you're coming to church with me, Benji! You will love it. The preacher is young and full of energy. I just love his sense of humor." Nancy buckled herself in and prattled all the way to the church.

As they walked in, Nancy held his arm possessively and introduced him to a group of ladies standing in the vestibule.

"I want you all to meet my son, Benji. Isn't he as handsome as I told you?"

The ladies all nodded and smiled.

"Hello, Benji, I'm Vera." Vera held out her hand and Ben shook it, surprised at the hard grip. For such a tiny woman she sure was strong. "We're glad to have you. I'm sorry for all that you've had to go through. We've all prayed and prayed for your recovery. Your mother is a true prayer warrior."

Ben wasn't surprised at all that they knew about his transplant. His mother loved to talk, especially about him. She probably told everyone she came in contact with. There was no sense in getting all bent out of shape about it. Telling her to stop would only be a waste of breath.

Ben thanked the ladies for their prayers and they slowly made their way to the pews. He sat down and immediately saw a woman a few rows directly ahead of him with long dark hair. He thought of the girl in his dreams. He was still having them. She was so beautiful and Ben was obsessed. He knew it was just a dream, but it felt so real.

Ben was lost in thought when his mother interrupted him. "You'll love the choir. They sing lots of old hymns but also bring out some new stuff that I've never heard of. I'm thinking of joining. I'm not the best singer in the world, but it's always nice to have lots of faces, and I can stand up there with a smile. I still have my teeth and I always like it when the choir is smiling and swaying like they're enjoying it and love the Lord."

Ben nodded absently while his mother talked on and on about the choir and joining a ladies Sunday school class. Ben barely listened; his attention was on the dark-haired girl. He wished she would turn her head so he could see her face.

The preacher finally stood up and welcomed everyone. The choir director led the choir in a hymn and then led everyone to shake hands. Ben watched the woman intently, willing her to turn around. She finally did, shaking hands with the older gentleman directly behind her. Ben sucked in his breath. It was her, the woman from his dreams. He wanted to get closer to see the blue of her eyes, but he couldn't leave the pew without stepping over everyone. His heart was pounding in his chest so loud he was sure his mother would hear.

Before they sat down, the girl looked directly at him and smiled. It was just an instant, but Ben felt his world rock. His head was spinning, his breath labored and his legs weak.

His mother whispered, "Are you okay, Benji? What's wrong?"

Trying to get control of himself, Ben took a deep breath and sat down. "I'm fine, Mom." He squeezed her hand and smiled. "Seriously, I promise."

Ben knew he had to meet her.

Chapter 11

A bby's pregnancy was beginning to show. Jenna made arrangements with the school so that Abby could finish her sophomore year with the homebound program. Jenna knew all of Abby's administrators and teachers personally. They would all work together to make sure Abby didn't fall behind. Her pregnancy was non-eventful so far, and Jenna prayed that it would stay that way.

Life was full speed ahead whether they were ready or not. Isaac made good on his promise and was with Abby every step. Abby made all her doctor's appointments in the afternoon so that he could go with her. The next appointment would let them know if it was a boy or girl.

Rachel talked Jenna into attending church with her one early spring morning. She had been real lazy about church and hated the thought of going without Craig. She had been a couple of times since his death, but she couldn't stand the look of pity on everyone's face. Rachel had been raving about the new preacher at her church and wanted Jenna to see for herself. By the look of the big crowd, it seemed a lot of people were excited about him. She heard they had a great daycare and was interested in checking it out as well. Hopefully they would have room for one more baby come fall.

Jenna had talked Abby into coming with her, and Abby had talked Katy into coming too for moral support. Abby was concerned that people would judge her since she was beginning to show. Rachel warned her that some people probably would but that was okay. Katy was one of the only real friends Abby had left.

After Abby and Isaac's friends found out about the pregnancy, social media had exploded. Thankfully, things were beginning to die down. Abby had handled it as well as she could, but sometimes Jenna saw the hurt in her eyes. Jenna had even felt herself being judged. She knew that people were saying it wouldn't have happened if Craig hadn't died, that somehow she was responsible.

After the choir sang an opening ensemble of older hymns, the preacher walked up to the pulpit and welcomed the congregation.

"I see we have a few new visitors this morning." He nodded towards a few people in the crowd including Jenna, Abby, and Katy. "We're glad to have you visit our church today and hope you come back." After relating a couple of news items, he asked everyone to greet those around them. Jenna was uncomfortable but she made herself shake hands with people in front of her and behind her. As she turned around, she noticed a man a few rows back staring intently at her. She was startled, but she smiled nervously. He was nice looking but a little thin and pale. An elderly lady beside him held his arm possessively. He didn't smile back, but he nodded slowly. Jenna turned around, shaken for some reason. She was breathing fast, and her heart was racing. What was wrong with her?

As they sat back down, Rachel looked at her funny. "Are you okay?"

Jenna nodded and smiled reassuringly but her mind was racing. Who was that man and why was he looking at her like that? And why was she shaking?

After the service, they walked slowly towards the vestibule and out the double doors where the preacher was shaking hands with everyone as they left the building. Rachel, Jenna, and Abby spoke to Preacher Jennings briefly and promised to all return the following Sunday. As they were walking towards the door, the man who had been staring at her during church bumped into her.

"Benji, watch where you're going." The older lady with him shook her head and then spoke to Jenna and Rachel. "So sorry, honey. Hi, my name is Nancy. Are y'all new here? This is my son's first time visiting too."

Jenna smiled. "Yes, this is our first visit." She looked towards Rachel. "My friend Rachel invited us. My name is Jenna, and this is my daughter Abby, and her friend Katy."

Abby took the opportunity to escape. "Mom, Katy and I are going to wait in the car." They were gone before Jenna had a chance to respond.

"Well, as I said, this is my son." Nancy turned to her son. "Benji is an engineer and he's single." She winked and smiled. Jenna could see red creeping up his neck, so she tried to ease the awkwardness of the situation by holding out her hand. "Hi, Benji, it's nice to meet you."

Ben held his hand out too, and she thought she detected a slight tremor. "Everyone but my mother calls me Ben. It's nice to meet you too." As soon as their hands touched, Jenna felt a warmth that she couldn't explain. She noticed that Ben was staring intently into her eyes and instead of feeling embarrassed, she felt drawn to him, which was very unusual for her.

Nancy turned to Rachel, seemingly oblivious. "How long have you been attending New Hope?"

While staring at Jenna and Ben, Rachel replied, "I've been coming here for a few months off and on." She turned finally to Nancy and said, "Preacher Jennings moved in next door from my condo. His wife, Carol, invited me."

Nancy nodded. "I just love Preacher Jennings and his wife! She and I go to a 'Crochet and More' class every Tuesday night. We have the best time; they're all so much fun. After Benji recovered..."

Ben interrupted his mother. "Mom, they're not interested in all that. It's time we left anyway unless you want to wait for a table at Nelly's. It was so nice meeting you both." Ben took Nancy's arm and ushered her towards the parking lot.

Once they were out of earshot, Rachel whispered, "Okay, what was that?"

Jenna shook her head, but she looked panicked. "Nothing, nothing at all."

Rachel gave her a look that suggested she didn't for one minute believe it was nothing.

Chapter 12

Ben sat on his small second-story deck, enjoying the North Carolina sunset. The sun was about to dip past the woods behind his apartment building. It was unusually warm, but another cold front was moving through in a couple of days, so he wanted to take advantage of the beautiful weather. He could hear the steady thump of a basketball and children playing on the playground. His mind kept going back to church and meeting Jenna. The warmth that passed through them as they shook hands was all he could think about. Even his mother commented on the 'spark' that passed between them. Oh, she didn't know that there really was a spark—just that they seemed to be taken with each other. She didn't pursue it though, which was unusual for her. Probably because her daughter, Abby, was possibly pregnant. Nancy never mentioned it, but in the car on the way to Nelly's she was quiet. Nancy was never quiet unless something pressing was on her mind.

He was still shocked that the girl plaguing his dreams was real. He met her, shook her hand, and stared into her blue eyes. He hadn't told anyone, not even Mark, his best friend. Mark would tell his wife, Lucy, and he just didn't want everyone knowing his business. He was getting tired of people looking at him with pity in their eyes.

How could he dream about someone he hadn't even met? Why did he feel such a connection toward her? Sure, she was beautiful, but it was more than that. He couldn't explain it and he was sure everyone would think he was crazy. He even felt something akin to affection for her daughter Abby. He loved Mark and Lucy's kids, but they were young and cute. Daniel was seven and Hannah was five. But Abby was a teenager.

Ben's phone alerted him to an incoming text message from Sarah. He hadn't heard from her since she came to tell him of her engagement. He thought about blocking her, but out of curiosity he opened up the message.

Hey Ben, I just wanted to let you know that I forgive you for the way you treated me. I've done a lot of soul searching and I have come to the conclusion that you're not angry at me but at the situation. Kip and I have set a date for our wedding this coming December. We would love for you and your mother to come. Kip has heard so much about you and would love to meet you both.

Ben knew that he was finally over Sarah because instead of getting mad he actually chuckled. How in the world did he put up with her as long as he did? She had done him a huge favor by breaking up with him. Sarah couldn't stand for anyone to be mad at her. He knew she would not let it go until he forgave her. He began typing a message and then stopped. Did he really forgive her? Did he want to give her and Kip his blessing? What kind of man has a name like Kip anyway? Ben pictured some skinny country club type. Probably couldn't even grow a mustache.

He typed *I'm glad you forgive me, and I hope you have a happy life with Kip, but I'm going to have to send my regrets....* Ben began backspacing, erasing everything, and then typed *K* and quickly pressed send before he changed his mind. He knew he should give her the closure she obviously needed but he just couldn't bring himself to do it. Yet.

The sun had set, and Ben decided to get up and clean up his dishes from dinner. He usually hand washed his dishes because it was something that soothed him in a monotonous sort of way. He liked to listen to music, hooking his phone up to a speaker so it sounded better. Lately he had been listening to more country music. He had never liked country music before, but on an impulse one day he typed George Strait on Pandora. He had been listening to it ever since.

He was almost finished when his phone rang. His sister, Laura, usually called on Sunday evenings. "Hey, sis, how's it going?"

Laura sighed. "My ear is sore. I've been on the phone with Mom, and she hardly took a breath from talking so much. Why does she think I want to hear about all these people I don't even know?" Ben chuckled but let her get it off her chest. "Who is this Vera and why is she telling me about Vera's neighbors and the problems she's having with cats peeing on her Nandinas, and what the heck are Nandinas?"

"It's a kind of bush I think."

"Well, whatever it is, it's beginning to smell like cat pee and it's turning brown in the process, in case you were wondering." She laughed and said, "Let's not waste our time talking about Vera and her Nandinas. How are you feeling?"

"I'm doing well."

"I guess you didn't get the talking gene from Mom. I want and need more than, *I'm doing well.* Give me the low down, Ben."

Ben loved his sister and really enjoyed their Sunday talks. She wouldn't admit it, but she got the talking gene from their mom. But she was always entertaining.

"I still don't have my energy back 100%, but I'm getting there. I was having a few pains, but the doctor assured me that it was normal."

"Have you heard anything else from Ding Dong?" *Ding Dong* was Laura's pet name for Sarah.

"Actually, she texted me earlier. Hold on and I'll copy it and send it to you." Once he copied, pasted, and sent it, he heard Laura gasp.

"Of all the nerve! How did you respond?"

"I was going to let her off the hook, and then the devil got a hold of me and I just texted *K.*"

Laura laughed out loud. "That's my big brother! Oh, how I miss you! Why don't you make plans to come out and see me? I promise I'll take some time off and show you around."

Ben had a hard time believing that whopper because he knew his sister was a workaholic and hardly ever took time off from work. She was the assistant to a very prominent producer in Hollywood. "Maybe. I've already taken so much time off from work, but I'll let you know. How are you, by the way? Are you still seeing Will?"

"Nah, we broke up. We just didn't have much in common." Laura paused and then continued, "To be honest, he was just really getting on my nerves, always wanting to go and go and go. After work, the last thing I want to do is go and go. You know what I mean? I just want to relax and I was tired of feeling guilty for it. Let him aggravate someone else."

Ben figured there was more to it than what she was saying but he let it go. "How's work?"

"Jack is as demanding as ever, but he's the best at what he does." Jack was her boss, and his production business was thriving. He was in constant demand. "He did give me a good raise. The cost of living out here is getting ridiculous, so I needed every penny." Laura talked more about her job while Ben finished up the dishes. He was lounging on the couch when she finally wrapped it up and said she needed to go. Her favorite take-out place was usually pretty busy on Sunday evening so she wanted to get her order in.

After they hung up, Ben got ready for bed. His mind went back to meeting Jenna. What would Laura say about it? She would probably think he was losing it. No, he would just keep his dreams to himself.

Chapter 13

Jenna took a personal day from work so she could take Abby to the gynecologist. Isaac was taking his Chemistry AP exam at school, and it wouldn't end until 4:00 that afternoon. Dr. Gorrell's office was located at the hospital. An ultrasound had been scheduled so they could possibly tell the gender of the baby if Abby wanted to know. Everywhere Abby went now, people tended to stare, making her self-conscience. She tried to wear baggy clothes, but her pregnancy was more and more obvious.

As Dr. Gorrell spread gel all over her abdomen, Jenna and Abby looked at the screen to see the images of the baby. At first, they couldn't make out anything. They finally saw the baby's profile, but it kept moving until the doctor exclaimed how active it was. He kept rolling the instrument around and Jenna's eyes grew wider. Abby said, "What, Mom? What do you see?"

The doctor smiled. "I believe it's pretty obvious what the gender is."

Jenna laughed. "Oh, my goodness!"

Abby lifted herself up on her elbows. "I can't see a thing. What is it?"

Jenna and the doctor looked at each other and he nodded. Tears began streaming down her face, but she finally whispered, "You've got yourself a little boy, Abby."

"A boy, really?"

Jenna nodded and then held Abby's hand.

They both cried and sniffed while the doctor finished his measurements and recorded the event. "It's a boy alright, and he looks healthy and by all measurements right on track."

Jenna said a quick thank you prayer. Abby had gained the normal amount of weight but was still pretty small. Jenna asked, "How much do you think the baby will weigh?"

Dr. Gorrell took his readers off and said, "I'd say about 7 or 7 1/2 pounds."

"Do you think she'll be able to deliver naturally?"

"As far as I know, but I'll be able to determine that closer to her due date, which is July 28."

Abby was hoping the baby would wait until July 30 which was Craig's birthday. Jenna thought she might feel different closer to the time. July was a pretty hot month, especially when you're pregnant.

Once Abby was dressed, they left the hospital and got milkshakes on the way home to celebrate. "I can't believe I'm having a boy." After a minute of silence, she said, "I wonder if he'll look like Dad." They didn't talk about Craig a lot, but he was always on their minds. "I've been thinking a lot about names, and I had thought if I was having a boy we could name him after Dad."

"You want to call him *Craig?*"

"No, Dad's name was *Samuel Craig*, right? But we'll call him Sam instead." Abby looked hopeful as if she very much wanted Jenna to love it as much as she did.

Jenna smiled. "I absolutely love it. Your daddy would be so proud."

* * *

Jenna and Rachel were having their Friday night get together. They were celebrating because school was almost finished. The students were all done testing and the teachers had a couple more workdays and then they were out for the summer. Isaac had graduated cum laude and had been accepted to UNC Chapel Hill. It was about a three-hour drive, but he promised to come home as much as he could. At least the baby would come before he left for school.

Rachel was so excited they were having a little boy. She was already calling herself Aunt Rachel. Jenna couldn't decide what she wanted to be called but had narrowed it down to Gigi, Mimi, or Gamma. She figured little Sam could make the final decision. They were going to look for baby furniture on Saturday. Craig's old office would become the nursery. They had already painted and put new carpet in it. All it needed now was baby stuff to put in it. There were a couple of secondhand baby stores in town, so they would check there first.

They had ordered loaded pizza with some kind of cinnamon bites for dessert that was scrumptious. Their bellies were full, so they were leaning back on the couch with their feet on the coffee table. Abby had gone over to Isaac's house to eat dinner with his family.

Rachel picked up her water bottle and took a sip and then clicked pause on the television remote. "I've got some news."

Just the way she said it had Jenna curious. "Well, spill the beans."

"I got a letter in the mail this week from the adoption agency." Jenna gasped as Rachel continued. "It basically said that my son wants to contact me if I approve."

"Oh, Rachel." Jenna's hand went to her mouth in surprise.

"I guess you know how I replied." Rachel shook her head. "I still can't believe it, after all these years." Jenna put her hand on Rachel's shoulder when big fat tears streamed down her best friend's face.

"I'm so scared though, Jenna. What if it doesn't go well? What if he decides that he doesn't want to contact me or worse, after he sees me, he changes his mind?"

"Rachel! That's crazy! Once he sees you, he'll love you, just like everyone else." It was true; Rachel had a personality that everyone loved. She was always fun and had everyone cracking up. During faculty meetings, she always entertained the staff, making something fun that would otherwise be tedious and sometimes boring.

Rachel closed her eyes. "But I did something that was unforgivable."

"Listen to me." Jenna took her hand and raised Rachel's face until she opened her eyes. "You did the only thing you could at the time. He's an adult, and he will understand. Okay? You can't worry about that."

Taking a deep breath, she nodded. "Yes, I know that. I did what I had to do at the time. Hopefully you're right. I was walking the other night and I saw the pastor's wife, Carol. We got to talking and I told her about him. I can't believe I did because hardly anyone knows it but somehow, I just spilled my whole life to her. Anyway, she was really sweet about it. She said she was happy to see you and Abby coming to church."

Jenna really enjoyed going to their church too, and not just because she got a glimpse of Ben every time she went. They hadn't really spoken again, just the usual *hey, how are you* stuff. She felt guilty every time she saw him because her heart began racing. She had already had the love of her life, and there wasn't room for a second one. Besides, her teenage daughter was pregnant, and Jenna was going to be a grandmother at 40.

"What do you think about Ben, Nancy's son?"

Because Ben had been on her mind, Jenna jumped guiltily. "Ben? Oh yeah, he's pretty nice. His mom likes to talk a lot."

Rachel had a smirk on her face. "I think you think he's more than pretty nice. Y'all are always trying to take a peek at each other."

"Oh pooh, I don't know what you're talking about." Jenna felt her face flooding with heat and knew she probably had red splotches on her neck. She took a big swig of her water, which turned into a messy gulp and then it spilled down her chin.

Jenna laughed, "Okay, yeah, you're right." Looking chagrined, she said, "I don't know what it is but there is something about him. I can't figure it out. He's cute but not drop-dead gorgeous."

"I knew it! His mother said he was single." Rachel raised her eyebrows. "Remember?"

"It doesn't matter anyway. I've only been a widow for seven months, and I'm going to be a grandmother in two months." She shook her head. "Ain't got time for that; Craig was it for me."

"Well, never say never. One day you may feel differently." Rachel clicked play so they could resume the Netflix documentary they had been watching.

Jenna picked it up and clicked pause again. "What about you? It's been two years since your divorce."

Rachel made a funny face and shook her head. "After what that jerk wad of a husband put me through last time, it will be a while before I go back down that road again." She clicked resume again but then changed her mind and clicked pause. "By the way, the jerk wad is getting married again."

"You're kidding, to whom?"

"Somebody he works with at the dealership. She sells cars too. I hope she knows what she's getting into." Rachel laughed. "Did I ever tell you that he sprayed his bald spot with hair color?" They both giggled. "One time it was really hot and humid and black streaks were dripping down the back of his neck." She took a deep breath. "We were married for 12 years, and I thought we were happy. I thought he loved me and I was a good wife to him. Once I lost my breasts though, it all changed. Even when I got new ones, he was still turned off."

Jenna didn't know what to say. They had had this conversation many times. Rachel still couldn't believe her husband had left her during such a horrible time of her life. Jenna wondered if she would ever get over it.

"But that's enough of that. Are you going to eat that last cinnamon thingy?" When Jenna shook her head, Rachel popped it in her mouth and gave a look that said she just tasted a little bit of heaven.

Chapter 14

Ben was standing in line at Starbucks waiting to buy some coffee. He had been to the hospital for a checkup and decided he needed a little treat before he went back to work. Even though it was hot outside, he still enjoyed his hot coffee. He heard the door chime and looked back absently. Jenna walked in and his heart did a flip flop, which was kind of dangerous for him. She smiled but looked a little embarrassed like she was wondering if she should turn back and run out the door. Slowly, she walked in until she was behind him in the line.

"Hey, Jenna, Jenna Rogers, isn't it? How's it going?"

"Hey, Ben, I'm well. How are you?"

"It's 90 degrees outside and I'm craving a hot coffee." He tried not to stare too intently at her, but it was really hard. His heart was racing, and he suddenly had the image of her pulling him toward her in the park and kissing him like his dream. Oh, boy, was he in trouble. Trying to think about anything else but kissing, he blurted out, "So how do you like New Hope?"

"I really enjoy Preacher Jennings. His sermons are very well put together. You can tell he really puts a lot of thought and time in them. What about you?"

Ben nodded. "I do enjoy them, a lot. Mom thinks she's dragging me every Sunday, but I secretly can't wait to go." Knowing Jenna was there put a little bounce in his step too. "Gives her something to brag about.

I'm just your average guy, but she feels like she's got the upper hand because her son brings her to church. She lords it over the other ladies." He winked and smiled.

Ben looked up when someone behind the counter cleared their throat and then realized he was next in line. He ordered his large black decaf coffee from the barista and paid with a generous tip. He then stepped out of the way so Jenna could order her drink. As they were waiting for their coffees, Ben asked Jenna if she was in a hurry and if she wanted to sit and talk for a bit.

Jenna hesitated for a second and he knew he was going to be turned down but instead she nodded and said, "Sure."

When their coffees were ready, they found a table and sat down awkwardly. Ben took one of the extra napkins he had and wiped some crumbs off into the floor. Jenna also had a hot coffee, but he could smell some kind of flavor—hazelnut maybe? Ben was the first to talk. "Are you from around here?"

Jenna took the lid off of her coffee and blew on it and then put her cup down. "I actually grew up in Cherryville just on the other side of the county."

Ben smiled. "I know where that is, and I know the locals get mad if you pronounce it wrong. It's Churrville, right?"

Jenna giggled and nodded. "Yep, my dad sold insurance there, but he died when I was younger. What about you?"

"I was born and raised in Belmont. My dad died when I was younger too. Massive heart attack."

"My dad had a brain aneurism."

Ben was silent for a moment and then said, "What brought you to Belmont?"

"My husband coached football at Cramer High School. I'm the Media Center director at Belmont Middle, or librarian as they used to call it. I remember your mother said you were an engineer. What kind of engineer?"

"I work for an architectural firm in Charlotte. You said your husband coached, as in past tense?"

Jenna took a deep breath and nodded. "Yes, he died last fall. A drunk driver hit him one night as he was coming home from a football game."

Ben sighed. "I'm so sorry, I didn't know."

Jenna nodded. "It's okay. It's still hard to talk about."

"Of course, again, I'm so sorry to even bring it up." Ben felt embarrassed but rambled on. "So, you have a daughter, her name is Abby?"

Jenna smiled. "Yes. Abby just turned 17. You probably noticed that she's pregnant. It was a real shock, but we're all dealing with it the best we can. Little Sam is due July 28."

"Wow! So, you're going to be a grandmother? You look way too young for that."

Jenna put the lid back on her coffee. "Well, sometimes we don't always get to choose these things. It's been a little strange, but we're all excited and looking forward to his birth. I just wish Craig were here. He would have been so excited." She stood up. "I guess I better get going."

Ben stood up too. He wanted to see her again but was afraid to ask. He grabbed his coffee and walked with Jenna to the door and out in the parking lot, trying to get up enough nerve to ask her out. Maybe it was too early for her to date. In the end he chickened out but promised himself that one day he would ask her. Talking to her felt so right, and he wanted to know everything about her. He didn't want to come across as being nosy, and she definitely looked like she scared easily. It may take some time, but one day soon he would get to know her.

Once Ben got to work and started up his computer, he hesitated but then typed in *Craig Rogers-football coach-car accident*. He saw the headlines *Beloved Coach Rogers Killed by a Drunk Driver*, and then his eyes grew wide when he saw that the date of the accident was three days before he received his new heart. Ben felt the blood rush to his face.

Chapter 15

Jenna got in her car, turned the engine on, and closed her eyes. When she had seen Ben in the coffee shop, she almost turned around and walked back out the door. She felt something every time she saw him and she could tell that he felt it too. She tried to tell herself that it was nothing, that it could happen with any attractive man. Craig had only been gone eight months; eight long months of missing him and trying to get on with her life. Abby's pregnancy, shock that it was, gave her something to look forward to. With her daughter being so young, Jenna had to take care of everything. Abby had really no idea how her life would change. Jenna would be there every step of the way, leading and guiding her. She prayed every day that everything would be okay. Little Sam was going to be a blessing in every way, she just knew it. He would make it all worth it; she only wished Craig was here to share it. He would be on top of the moon once he got over the shock of it.

Jenna could still smell Ben's cologne. It was a subtle but familiar scent. She liked it. She liked his dark brown hair and the way it curled slightly at his ears. It was a little long, but she liked it that way. His eyes were grayish green and they sparkled when he talked. And that wink—that wink just about did her in. Ben had a deep, husky voice and beautiful white, straight teeth. It seemed he got better looking every time she saw him. He looked nothing like Craig, but something about him reminded her of Craig.

Jenna was so deep in thought that when her cell phone rang, she jumped, feeling guilty. What was wrong with her, ogling over a man she barely knew and had no business thinking about? She saw Rachel's name pop up.

"Hey, what's up?"

"Have I got a story to tell you. Where are you?"

"I just got some coffee and was getting ready to head home."

"Can you swing by my condo? I promise you won't be disappointed."

"Sure, I'm on my way."

Rachel lived in a two-bedroom condominium close to town. She bought it after her divorce. It was nice, affordable, and close to a great greenway, which they both liked to take advantage of.

The door was unlocked, so Jenna walked in. Rachel wasn't in the living room. She hollered, "Where are you? You've got me curious." She heard a toilet flush and then Rachel walked in grinning.

"Want something to drink?"

Jenna held up her coffee. "No, I would have gotten you one, but I'd already left."

"I've still got some coffee in the pot. Hold on while I fix a cup."

Jenna sat down on the couch. Rachel's cat, Bubba, was in a chair staring with evil in his eyes. Jenna knew if she made one wrong move, he would pounce and scare her to death. He was without a doubt the most hateful cat that ever lived. She could hear a low menacing growl and tried to look everywhere but at him.

"Cut it out, Bubba." Rachel shooed him and he jumped off the chair and sauntered slowly out of the living room. "Dumb cat. He threw up on my bed this morning." She held up her fingers. "He's this close to going to the pound." She said it loudly as if Bubba would understand her and straighten his ornery self up.

Jenna laughed because she knew it was all talk. Rachel always threatened to take him to the pound. She loved him for some odd reason.

Rachel put her coffee cup down. "So, you know I told you that Roger Smith asked me out?" Roger was a math teacher from another middle school in the county. They got to talking at one of the math curriculum meetings, and Rachel said he seemed like he was a lot of fun. "He has a pontoon boat and we took it out on the lake. Everything was going pretty good. He likes to talk a lot about NASCAR, though, and I don't know any of the drivers now. The only ones I remember are Richard Petty and Darrell Waltrip. Anyway, he gets this funny look, and he says he's really sorry, but he has to go. There's no bathroom on the boat but there is a bucket." She closed her eyes and put her hand on her mouth for a dramatic effect. "Well, he pooped in a bucket."

Jenna's eyes widened. "What?"

"Yes." Rachel nodded. "He pooped in a bucket." Jenna couldn't help but laugh. "Needless to say, that was it for me. When he took me home, he said that he really had a good time and wanted to see me again, but all I could think about was him pooping in that bucket. I didn't actually see him pooping in the bucket, but you know I have a very vivid imagination." After taking a deep breath she continued. "When I didn't say I wanted to see him again, he asked me if it was because he 'used the bucket' and I lied and said, 'No, of course not.' I mean, really, how could I be that shallow? But I guess I am. I could see if we had been married or even dated for a while, but on our first date? Really, he can't wait?"

Jenna nodded. "Yeah, that's pretty bad."

Rachel held her mug up with both hands and blew the coffee and then instead of taking a drink, she set it back down. "What if I had to go? Would he mind if I pooped in the bucket? Never mind that I would hold it until I came close to messing my pants." Rachel closed her eyes and shook her body with revulsion. "Every time I see him now, that's what I'm going to think about. Definitely one of the worst dates ever. Has to go up from there, right?"

Jenna laughed again. "I dated a guy in high school that pulled his car over on the side of the road and peed on a tree."

Rachel held up her finger. "My question is, did you date him again?"

"No." Jenna looked thoughtful and said, "I'm not sure if it was that he peed on a tree or that he made me pay for my food. We went to a food truck that was in the K-Mart parking lot. He got in line and got his food first, paid for it, and then walked over to the pickup line. I stood there stupidly at first, not sure what to do. Thankfully, I had enough cash to buy a burrito and a Coke."

"I'm seriously considering getting on a dating website." Jenna shook her head but Rachel continued. "No, really, I've been seeing a bunch of commercials. There's even one for Christians."

"Just be careful. You hear of these horror stories about women sending money to these men until they're broke and living in their cars and then their kids are all mad."

"I think I'm smarter than that." Rachel sipped her coffee and leaned back on the sofa. "Mary Wilson met her husband that way. They seem happy enough." Mary was the receptionist at the school where they both worked. She was in her 50s and looked like she was in her 70s. "If she can find a fella, then surely I can."

"Poor Mary, I don't know how she survives each day." Jenna grimaced. "I had to help watch the front office one day when she was out sick. All I did was take messages for parents to give to their kids." Dramatically, Jenna said, "Tell Johnny to ride the bus today; let Mary know I'm coming to bring her cheer outfit after school; Timmy's not feeling good today, make sure he has his sweater on. Oh, and my favorite, tell Kevin when he gets home, he better not eat the leftover steak in the fridge. He had his last night." Jenna closed her eyes. "I swear, I would kill myself if I had to be a school secretary every day."

Rachel laughed. "I know! Usually, the whole front office is full of shoes, socks, sports equipment, and who knows what else. It's like a revolving door with parents dropping stuff off. You can't even walk through there sometimes."

Suddenly, Rachel looked serious. "I got a letter today."

Jenna smiled. "You're kidding."

"It was short but interesting." Rachel bit her lip. "Want to read it?"

Jenna nodded and Rachel retrieved it from her back pocket, handing it to her. *My name is Jason, and I have reason to believe that you're my birth mother. Below is my email address. Can you contact me so that we may correspond that way?*

Jenna looked up at Rachel and then placed her hand on her best friend's shoulder. "Oh, my, it's really happening. You are going to contact him, right?"

Rachel nodded. "I'm so nervous, though. I have no idea what to say."

Jenna smiled reassuringly. "It will all be fine, Rachel. I'm so happy for you."

Jenna felt her phone vibrate and took it out of her pocket and gasped.

Rachel put her hand on Jenna's knee. "What is it? What's happened?"

Jenna stood up to leave. "Abby just texted and said she's having contractions and they won't stop. I've gotta go."

Rachel stood up. "Well, I'm going with you." Both women grabbed their purses and ran out the door.

Chapter 16

Nancy was waiting on the porch when Ben pulled in the driveway. She was opening the car door before he pulled to a complete stop. "Are you in a hurry, Mom?"

"I just don't want to be late." She put her purse on her lap and then locked her seatbelt. "They're having a baptism today. You know there are always a lot more people during a baptism. I want to make sure I get my spot."

Ben shook his head and put the car in reverse. "Would it be a bad thing if you didn't get your spot?"

Nancy pursed her lips. "I'm sure I would live, but I see better from where I usually sit. I can see the preacher and the choir good and that's where my friends sit. They may think I'm mad or something if I don't sit with them."

Ben sighed. "So how was your day yesterday? Did you go out with Larry?"

"Yes."

Ben looked at his mother who was staring straight ahead. "Well, how did it go?"

"It was fine. We had an early dinner and then we went for a walk in the park before he took me home."

Ben could tell that something was bothering his mom, but he figured she would let him know sooner or later. Apparently it would be sooner.

"Laura called me after I got home last night."

Here we go. Ben prepared himself for a long narrative of their entire conversation.

"I asked Laura when she was coming back home for a visit. She hasn't been home in two years, which is hard enough, but not coming in for her only brother's surgery is unforgivable. Of course, she got mad at me. I just don't understand her. I know how much it hurt you when she didn't come home to see you."

Ben shook his head, but Nancy continued on her tirade.

"She gets mad at me when I ask her anything. I asked about her fella, Will, and she got in a tizzy about it. Then, when she wouldn't talk, I was just talking to fill the quiet, and she got mad about that. I was telling her about Mr. Blevins, my neighbor that lives down the street, about his little three-legged dog biting Mrs. Hall that lives across the street from him. Poor Mrs. Hall had to go to the emergency room to get a couple of stitches and Mr. Blevins didn't even bother to pay the bill. Well, Laura just hollered and said she didn't give a you-know-what about my neighborhood drama and if that's all I wanted to talk about then she would call back another time and hung up on me!" Nancy stopped long enough to take a tissue out of her purse. "I just don't know what I ever did to deserve to be treated like that." She wiped her eye and blew her nose. "What kind of mother would I be if I didn't want to ever see my children? Of course I want to see her and then she gets mad about it." She pushed the visor down and looked at herself in the mirror. "Now look; my makeup is running." She took a compact out of her purse and began dabbing under her eyes.

Ben knew his mother and sister had had a difficult relationship ever since Laura was a teenager. It seemed that he was always trying to be a mediator even when he was young and didn't know what a mediator was; especially since his dad died. Laura was always close to their dad and his mom was always a little jealous of their relationship. "Mom, try not to take it personally. Laura loves you; she's just having a rough time right now. I think her job and all the hours she's putting in are really getting to her."

As they pulled into the parking lot at church, Nancy turned to Ben. "Of course she is; that's why I want her to take a break and come home."

They both unbuckled their seat belts and got out of the car. On the way, Ben put his arm around his mom's shoulders. "Try not to worry. Laura will surprise you one day when you least expect it."

Nancy found her spot in her favorite pew that was thankfully still vacant and began talking to her friends. Ben looked around to see if Jenna was sitting in her usual spot, but instead he saw Rachel by herself. Rachel smiled and waved as if she knew it wasn't her he was looking for but her friend. Ben smiled back and nodded.

After church, as Ben and his mother were walking to his car, Rachel walked up to them. "Hey, how's it going?"

Nancy spoke first. "We're doing well..." Nancy stopped because she couldn't remember her name.

"Rachel."

"Yes, Rachel. Sorry about that, my mind isn't as good as it used to be. Wasn't that a wonderful baptism? It's not often you see a parent and a child get baptized at the same time. I couldn't help but chuckle when little Jeremy dunked himself before the preacher could do it." They all laughed.

Before they could leave, Rachel said, "I just wanted to let you know that Jenna and Abby couldn't be here today. Abby has been having contractions and is on bed rest. She was in the hospital for about five days, but they stopped her labor, thank goodness. Hopefully she can hold out for a few more weeks."

Nancy gasped. "Oh, my, I'll add her to the prayer chain. Is her mama okay?"

"She's really worried, but I think she's okay."

Nancy nodded. "I know how it is to be worried. When Benji was in the hospital waiting on a new heart last October, I was a nervous wreck because I knew it would take a miracle for him to get one, but our prayers were answered and Benji is standing here today." She took his arm and squeezed it. "I just don't know what I would do without him."

Ben felt Rachel's curious gaze and smiled uncomfortably, trying to change the subject. "Please let Jenna and Abby know that we're praying for them. We hope everything goes well with the baby."

Rachel nodded. "I will. I knew that she would want y'all to know."

Once Ben and his mom were in the car and headed to lunch, Nancy shook her head. "I can't believe that young girl is pregnant. Why, she hardly looks like she's 15."

"She's 17."

Nancy glanced quickly at Ben. "How do you know how old she is?"

"I saw Jenna at the coffee shop one day and we talked a bit."

"Really?" Ben nodded and then Nancy said, "Is she married?"

Ben stopped at a traffic light. For some reason he was hesitant to talk about Jenna but instead he said, "Jenna's a widow." The light turned green and Ben pulled forward. "Are we still going to Jackson's Cafeteria?"

"Yes, I'm craving a vegetable plate. How long has Jenna been a widow?"

Ben lied for some reason and said, "I'm not sure." Thankfully they finally made it to the parking lot of the restaurant. Ben hoped that would end the conversation. He didn't want to talk about what he knew about Jenna and her husband, Craig, and that Ben had received a new heart when Craig died. He was still trying to grapple with this knowledge and losing sleep over it. Did dreaming about Jenna before he had even met her have something to do with his new heart? If he did have Craig's own heart beating in his body, was that why he had such a connection to Jenna? Ben knew there was no other explanation. It had to be.

Chapter 17

Jenna was in the kitchen fixing lunch. Abby was getting cranky from having to stay in bed so much that Jenna begged Rachel to come over and eat with them. They were going to watch *Pride and Prejudice* and eat chicken salad on butter croissants, which she couldn't resist buying at the grocery store. Jenna had brought a blanket and put it on Craig's recliner for Abby. Hopefully, Abby would get in a better mood. Rachel could always make her laugh. They all needed a few laughs after the trauma of Abby's pre-labor. Jenna had never been so scared in all her life. What they thought were Braxton Hicks contractions became more serious. She was sent to the hospital and the doctor had placed her on magnesium, which stopped the labor, but in the process, Abby had lost all use of her body. Seeing her daughter so out of it, not able to speak or move, was the most scared she had ever been for her child. Isaac came to the hospital, but after seeing Abby in that condition, it was just too much for him, so he left. Jenna, with Rachel's help, stayed with Abby day and night, because she was scared and didn't want to be left alone. She had been home for about a week, and the monotony was beginning to get to Abby.

Jenna was stirring the sugar in the tea jug when she heard Rachel come in the kitchen door. "Thank goodness you're here. Abby is about to drive me crazy."

"Why is she crazy? She's got the internet, Netflix, and TikTok." Rachel hung her purse on the coat rack next to the door. "I wish I could sit all day and watch TikTok. When they show those pimple popping videos, I cringe, but I can't look away! It's a sickness."

Jenna shook her head in disgust. "How could you watch that? That's gross!"

Rachel looked serious. "I told you it's a sickness." She picked up one of the glasses of tea Jenna had prepared and sipped, peeping over the top of the glass to gauge Jenna's reaction. "I saw Ben and his mother at church yesterday."

Jenna tried to not act like she was interested but failed miserably. "So, how are they?"

"I told them about Abby, and Nancy said she would add her to the prayer chain."

"That's nice, anything else?"

Rachel smiled. "Ben wanted to make sure I told you that you're in his prayers and he hopes everything goes well with the baby."

Jenna took a sip of her tea. "He said that I'm in his prayers?"

"Well, I think he said that they're praying for you both, something like that."

"Hmmmm." Jenna tried to look like she wasn't dying to know everything Ben said or did.

"He looked real good too. He sure knows how to dress. His suits always fit him perfectly and I love his style in ties."

Jenna busied herself with the sandwiches. "Well, maybe you should ask him out. I bet he won't poop in a bucket."

Rachel laughed. "No, I'm pretty sure he wouldn't do that." Rachel tapped her chin. "How could I ask him out when you two are always making googly eyes at each other?"

"We do not make 'googly eyes' at each other, for goodness sakes."

"Why are you turning red, Jenna?"

"I'm not turning red. It's very warm today. It's at least 90 degrees outside." Jenna busied herself putting the rest of the chicken salad on the croissants, trying not to let Rachel's teasing get to her.

"Hmmmm." Rachel mimicked Jenna. "Well, anyway, what are we watching today?"

"*Pride and Prejudice*, the one with Keira Knightley." Jenna picked up the platter of sandwiches and handed it to Rachel. "Can you put these on the coffee table? I'll bring in the chips and fruit plate."

Rachel stopped Jenna. "Before we do, can I ask you a question?"

Jenna nodded and Rachel continued. "Did you ever find out who got Craig's organs?"

Jenna, looking surprised, shook her head. "No. I don't think I want to know. I just think it would be awkward. Why?"

Rachel took the platter to the living room and called over her shoulder. "No reason. I was just wondering."

Jenna hollered at Abby when everything was in place. "Abby, lunch is ready!"

Abby slowly waddled into the living room and got in the recliner. She looked pale and bloated. She had a lot of water retention in her legs, and they looked twice their original size. She had her phone with her, and a sulking look on her face. "Isaac won't return my texts."

Jenna tried to reassure her. "He's at the beach with his parents. I'm sure he doesn't have his phone on him 24/7."

"His child could be born, like, any minute. I can't believe he went to the beach while I'm stuck here and can't even do anything."

Rachel and Jenna both looked at each other, and Rachel could tell by the look on Jenna's face that she had about had it. Rachel decided to stir the pot. "You got that right. He's got some nerve leaving and having a good time while you're in such misery."

"I know! It's not fair!" Abby stuck her bottom lip out like a child. Chip, who had been sleeping contently on the sofa, jumped off the couch and headed towards the bedroom where it was quiet.

Rachel held out her hand. "Give me your phone. I'll let him know what a jerk he's being."

Abby looked taken aback. "What?"

Rachel pointed her finger. "He needs to know how you feel."

Abby shook her head. "No. I don't want to do that."

Jenna and Rachel looked at each other and Jenna shrugged. Rachel sat down on the corner of the couch next to Abby's chair.

"Abby, I'm so sorry for all you're going through. I know it's been tough. You're miserable and scared and your boyfriend is on vacation having a grand time."

Jenna walked over and handed Abby a glass of iced tea and watched Rachel try to help her daughter.

"Pretty soon you're going to have this wonderful little baby boy and he's going to have so much love. Your mom, me, Isaac and his family, and your grandparents will all love him. Your daddy is watching in heaven and he's making sure that you're going to be okay."

At the mention of Craig, Abby broke down and sobbed, putting her face in her hands. Jenna got on her knees and gently stroked her back, tears rolling down her face too.

Through her sobs, Abby cried, "I miss Daddy so much."

"I know, sweetie. It's not fair that he's gone, but he wouldn't want you and your mom so upset and crying. He would want you to be happy and looking forward to seeing little Sam." Rachel tipped Abby's face up. "Right?"

Abby nodded and sniffed loudly. Jenna couldn't stand it anymore, so she made an excuse of checking on 'something in the kitchen.' After a few minutes of crying softly to herself, Rachel came in to check on her. She turned and wiped her eyes discreetly.

"I'm fine, so quit giving me that look." Jenna opened a cabinet door but just stood there looking blankly into the cupboard.

"You don't look so fine to me."

Jenna sighed heavily. "It's been a little rough, but it will all be fine." After seeing Rachel's disbelieving face, she tried to smile.

Instead of arguing, Rachel decided to change the subject and try to bring a 'real' smile to Jenna's face. "So, I heard back from Jason."

Rachel had responded to her son's first email letting him know that she definitely wanted to correspond with him but didn't hear back from him right away. Jenna knew that Rachel was hurt but trying not to show her disappointment. "Oh, my goodness, what did he say?"

"He lives in Charlotte!"

"You're kidding me!"

"He's a web designer and works for some medical group designing their websites. Can you believe it?"

Jenna's hand was over her mouth. "I can't believe it! That's crazy."

"We'll talk about it more later." Rachel pointed outside the kitchen window. "I found the crib Abby wanted. I went ahead and picked it up and it's in the back of my car. Let's go tell her."

Jenna nodded gratefully. "Are you going to put it together too?"

Rachel shook her head. "Afraid not, you know I'm too impatient to read directions."

"Maybe Bill could come over and help," Jenna wondered out loud. Craig's parents were always offering to help with anything they could. They weren't in the best of health, but Jenna would ask.

Rachel grinned sheepishly. "Maybe a certain snappy dresser can come over and help you?"

Jenna scoffed. "I doubt it." Jenna began walking towards the living room, effectively closing the subject. "Let's eat. I'm starving."

Jenna and Abby watched the movie, but Rachel was thinking about what Ben's mother had told her. She wondered if it was possible that Ben had received Craig's heart. It seemed a long shot, but the dates fit perfectly. It was just speculation, though, and she decided not to say anything to her friend. Jenna had enough on her mind.

Chapter 18

Ben woke up with a start. He had been dreaming of Jenna again. He was shaving and she had walked up behind him and put her arms around him. He looked at her through the bathroom mirror and her smile was full of love and promise. He was lost in her gaze and then he saw himself; but it wasn't him, it was someone else. Ben shook his head and upper body. Why would he have a dream like that? What did it mean if anything?

He slowly got out of bed. He hurt all over. He had been going back to the gym to get back into shape. They were very light workouts but after not doing anything for so long it didn't take much to make his muscles burn and scream in pain. He was determined to get through it, whatever it took.

Unfortunately, he ran into Sarah at the gym. Feeling he hadn't treated her well, he decided he needed to apologize. She had just gotten off the treadmill and was wiping her face and neck. She seemed surprised and wary that he had approached her.

"I'd like to apologize for the way I acted, Sarah." When she didn't respond, he continued. "I shouldn't have taken my frustrations out on you, and it was wrong of me."

Sarah nodded. "I accept your apology. You were very nasty to me, but I understand that you've had a rough time."

"Okay then." Ben pointed toward the stationary bikes. "I'll get back to it."

Sarah stopped him. "Ben?"

Ben had already turned away, but hearing her say his name caused his shoulder's to sag because he had almost gotten away. He turned back to face Sarah. "Yeah?"

Sarah hesitated. "You...you really look great."

"Thanks. I'm beginning to get back to my old self, I think."

"I just never thought you would pull through. You were dying and now... and now look at you." Sarah bit her bottom lip. "I never meant to hurt you, Ben, you know that, right?"

Ben thought about the night Sarah told him she just couldn't deal with his illness and the thought of him dying. He thought his damaged heart would break in two or just disintegrate. He needed her, and after she left, he thought he really didn't have much to live for. "I know in your own way, you did what you thought you had to do."

Sarah tried to explain. He had heard it before, and he really wasn't interested, but he let her talk. "I was so scared, Ben. I loved you so much and l wanted to leave you before you left me."

"So you said."

"It's true, Ben. I loved you, I still love you." She held out her hand towards him, but he just looked at it. Ben didn't know what to say. He remembered a time that if he had heard those words, he would have leapt for joy. Now, he wondered what she wanted. How would her fiancé feel if he knew that Sarah was telling her ex-husband that she still loved him? Ben didn't believe it anyway.

"What do you want me to say, Sarah?"

Sarah's hand awkwardly dropped. "I don't know."

"Be happy, Sarah. You're getting married in December, right?" When Sarah nodded, Ben smiled. "Think about your future, not the past. I'm in a great place in my life now, so don't worry about me." Ben pointed to the bikes again. "Look, I really need to get busy or I'm going to be late for work. Take care." Ben hurried through his workout still puzzling over Sarah.

On the way to work, his mother called. "Benji, are you on your way to work?" Hardly waiting for him to answer, she continued, "Can you stop by on your way home this evening? My computer is messed up. I have a feeling that it's past fixing so maybe we can go out soon and you can help me pick out another one." She rambled on and on for about five minutes until he heard her mention Rachel and about giving her his number.

"You what?"

"I gave Rachel your phone number. She said she needed to talk to you about something, something about your job. I hope it's okay. She talked to the pastor's wife, Carol, to get my number."

"That's fine. Don't worry."

"Sounds kind of fishy to me. Maybe she's going to ask you on a date, but I can see you only have eyes for Jenna, am I right?"

"Mom, Jenna just lost her husband, and her daughter is about to give birth to a baby. She hardly has time for a new boyfriend."

"Which tells me that you've definitely thought about it."

Ben interrupted his mother. "Mom, please stop. I'm just about to turn into the parking lot. I'll come by this evening and look at your computer."

"Text me and let me know when you're on the way so I can have dinner ready for you. I love you, sweetheart."

"I love you too."

Ben put his car in park and rubbed his face and wondered what Rachel wanted to talk to him about.

She called him an hour later. She said she realized he was at work, but could he call her when he got a break, maybe during lunch? He decided to grab some takeout, so he called as soon as he got in his car.

"Rachel? It's Ben Thompson."

"Hey, Ben, thanks for calling me back."

"No problem. What can I help you with?"

Rachel hesitated. "Um, well, I've got something on my mind, and I can't rest until I ask you about it." Ben knew what she was going to ask. "Your mother said you had a heart transplant last October, right?"

"Yes. I did. I have a feeling I know what you're going to ask. I have no idea if I received Jenna's husband's heart, but I did receive a new heart three days after he was in the wreck. Did they donate his organs?"

"Yes, they did, three days after the wreck. Wow. This is very interesting." Rachel was quiet as they both were lost in thought. "Jenna has no idea who received his organs. She doesn't know that you had a heart transplant last October either."

"Can I ask a favor, Rachel? Can you please not tell her?"

There was a moment of silence and then Rachel said, "Jenna is my best friend, Ben. I can't keep secrets from her."

"I know. I'm sorry to ask you to keep something from her, but do we even know for sure that I did receive his heart?"

"Why don't you want her to know?" When Ben was silent, Rachel said, "You like her, don't you?"

For some reason, Ben was afraid to talk about his feelings for Jenna, but he finally relented. "Yes. I do like her, Rachel. A lot."

"I see."

Ben tried his best to tell Rachel how he felt and how he was afraid. "Look, I know Jenna is very vulnerable right now. It's only been a few months since she lost her husband, and her teenage daughter is about to give birth to a baby. I don't want to scare her or make her feel uncomfortable around me. You know she's not ready for that and I'm willing to wait as long as it takes to get to know her. Can you just please give me some time? I promise I'll tell her."

Ben prayed silently while he waited for Rachel's answer. "Okay, but I don't feel right about it. If she finds out that I knew and didn't tell her, she is not going to be happy with me and I wouldn't hurt her for the world."

Ben sighed in relief. "Thank you, Rachel."

"Don't make me regret this."

"I won't. How are Jenna and Abby?"

"Abby is cranky and Jenna is exhausted worrying about her. It shouldn't be long now."

"Can you let me know when Abby has the baby?"

"Sure. Look, I've got to go. Thanks for calling me back."

* * *

Later that evening, Nancy had dinner on the table when Ben arrived. "I made one of your favorites, chicken and rice casserole."

"Looks great, Mom, thanks."

Nancy poured him some iced tea and put it in front of his plate and sat down. As soon as Ben blessed the food, his mom said, "Did you hear from Rachel today?"

Ben knew it was coming sooner or later. He took his napkin and laid it on his lap stalling for time. "Yeah."

"Well, what did she want?" Nancy sat down and took a sip of her tea, waiting expectantly.

"She was asking about my job."

"Your job? What did she want to know?"

Ben closed his eyes and sighed, wondering what it would be like to have a mom who wasn't nosy and inquisitive all the time. "She wanted to know if they were hiring." He tried to eat but Nancy wouldn't let it go.

"Hiring? Is she looking for a job?"

"No, but she knows someone who is."

"Who?"

Suddenly Ben's temper flared. "Good grief, Mom, I don't know. Somebody she knows."

"You don't have to get all hateful."

Ben knew he hurt her feelings because she suddenly became quiet. Trying to appease her, he began eating with gusto. "This is so good. Thanks for cooking."

She picked up her napkin and wiped her mouth. "You're welcome."

"So, what's going on with your computer?"

Nancy stood up with her plate and took it to the sink, scraping off her uneaten food. "It just keeps freezing."

"How old is it?"

"About 10 years."

"Yeah, you probably need another one. I'm sure it's outdated and out of memory. Maybe we can go Sunday after we eat lunch and look for a new one."

"That's fine."

"Look, Mom, I'm sorry I snapped at you. It's been a long day. Work was extremely busy and I'm still trying to play catch up." Nancy was still standing at the sink with her back to Ben, her head down. Ben got up and hugged her from behind. "I can be a real jerk sometimes."

Nancy put her hand on Ben's hand. "It's okay, sweetie."

Once he was sure his mom had gotten over her pouting spell, Ben left for home. He was gathering up his shirts to drop off at the dry cleaners the next day when he got a text from Rachel.

Abby has checked into the hospital. It won't be long.

Chapter 19

Jenna looked at her new grandson in awe. He was absolutely perfect—a little small, but perfect. Abby's contractions came fast and strong, but she never dilated. The doctor waited as long as possible, but little Sam was showing signs of stress, so they decided to do a cesarean. Abby wanted to have the baby on Craig's birthday, but he wouldn't wait.

"Can I hold him now?"

Jenna nodded and handed the baby to Abby. "Make sure you support his head."

"I know," Abby said irritably. She placed him on the pillow that covered her stomach. "Isn't he beautiful?" Her fingers traced his sweet little face as she smiled, her love shining brightly in her eyes.

Jenna nodded. "Yes. He's perfect." She busied herself by straightening up the hospital room so she wouldn't make Abby nervous. Once she was done, she sat down in one of the provided chairs and watched her daughter and grandson. "You sure you don't want to try and feed him again?"

Abby shook her head. "No. I tried, Mom, but I just don't feel comfortable. The nurse said that the baby formula would be fine." Sam was sleeping peacefully while Abby petted and cooed to her son.

Jenna nodded. She and Abby had discussed breastfeeding before the baby was born, but Abby didn't sound too convinced. She said she would try it, although Jenna could see it was only halfheartedly.

"Have you heard from Isaac?" Isaac had been with Abby during the birth but had gone home to get some rest. His parents, Jenna's mom, Craig's parents, and Rachel had all been at the hospital waiting on Sam to be born.

"Isaac said he was coming in a little bit. He's bringing me a cheeseburger, fries, and a big ole Coke."

Jenna smiled. "I'm going to go home and get some clothes for you to come home in. Is there anything in particular you want me to bring?"

Before Abby could respond, they heard a soft knock on the door. Jenna looked up and saw Ben walk in smiling, holding a bunch of blue balloons and a gift basket.

"If it's a bad time, I can come back later."

Jenna was a little shocked to see him. "How did you know?"

"Rachel told me." He placed the basket on the windowsill edge and stood holding the balloons sheepishly.

Jenna looked at Abby to make sure it was okay, but Abby was smiling. She held up her baby proudly. "This is Sam. Isn't he adorable?"

Ben walked over towards the bed and peered down. "He's a handsome fella alright." Ben touched Sam's cheek with his finger. "Everyone okay?"

Sam squirmed and made little grunting noises and then passed some gas. They all laughed and Abby said, "Well, he's a little gassy, but other than that, we're all fine." She adjusted his blanket and then tucked him against her breast.

Ben tied the balloons to one of the chairs. "The gift basket is from me and my mother who, by the way, says hello and congratulations. She's been crocheting like crazy so she could get the blanket finished."

Jenna peeked at the blue basket which had all sorts of baby items nestled in a beautiful, crocheted baby blanket. "That's so nice, Ben. Thank you." She couldn't believe Ben was at the hospital and bringing gifts. It was the last thing she expected. She felt so drawn to him and had the urge to hug him. When he looked at the baby, his eyes were shining as if he was holding back tears.

"My mom is crazy about babies and hopes that you'll let her hold him at church." He chuckled. "Of course, she may talk his ears off."

Jenna giggled. "Well, between your mom and my mom, his little ears don't have a chance."

Ben clasped his hands and said, "I guess I better go. I just wanted to bring the gifts by and take a peek at the baby. Mom wants all the details." Ben suddenly looked serious. "By the way, how much does he weigh, how long is he, and what's his full name?" He laughed at the expression on Jenna and Abby's faces. "Just kidding. No, really, Mom wants to know." They all laughed as he walked towards the door.

Before he could leave, Isaac came in with a bag of fast food and two huge drinks. Jenna stood up. "Hey, Isaac, this is Ben. Ben is a friend of ours from church." She looked at Abby. "I'm going to walk out with Ben and head home to get your stuff. Text me if there is anything in particular you need."

As they walked quietly towards the elevators, Jenna got a whiff of Ben's cologne. He smelled so good. He was dressed in black slacks and a white buttoned shirt that fit him perfectly. She could tell that he had put on a little more weight and was looking better every time she saw him. They stepped into the elevator, and before the door could close, a large group walked in, so Ben and Jenna scooted to the back. They were standing so close that their clothes were touching. Someone bumped slightly into Jenna, pushing her even closer to Ben. Their hands were touching and then she felt Ben's hand gently grasp hers. She was so shocked that she froze. Ben looked straight ahead as if it was normal for them to hold hands. Before she knew it, the elevator stopped at the main level. Everyone stepped out including Ben and Jenna, their hands gradually drifting apart.

Ben cleared his throat. "Do you have time to grab some coffee in the cafeteria before you go home?"

Not wanting to part with him so soon, Jenna nodded. "Sure, sounds good."

Ben paid for their coffee, and they found a small table in the busy cafeteria. "Sam really is a beautiful baby. I know you must be so proud."

"Yes, it was a shocker when I found out Abby was pregnant, but now I'm so happy he's here. I know she doesn't really have a clue about raising a baby, but I know it will all be okay. God had a different plan than what we all imagined for sure." She took a tentative sip of her hot coffee. "Thank you again for the gift. Please tell your mom we said thank you. By the way, his name is Samuel Craig, he weighed 6.2 pounds, and he's 20 inches long." They both laughed and then Jenna cleared her throat. "So, as you noticed, Isaac is... not white." Jenna took a deep breath. "I feel so funny saying that. I'm not sure how to go about relaying the information that Sam is biracial without sounding racist."

Ben looked at Jenna in understanding. "I also noticed how beautiful Sam is and how perfect. I know you're very proud."

Jenna smiled in relief. "I am proud. Abby did so well, and Isaac was such a trooper. I had no idea how it would go with them being so young." Jenna looked down, almost embarrassed by the intent stare of Ben's eyes.

"When do you have to go back to work?"

Jenna fidgeted with her napkin. "Our workdays start the second week in August. School will begin about a week after that."

"Will Abby go back to school?"

"Yes. She may wait a week or two after school officially begins. She had a cesarean, and it takes a little longer to heal. She's young, though, and will bounce back pretty fast. I wasn't sure if she was ready, but she says she's excited about going back."

"Who's going to watch the baby?"

"The church has a daycare." She smiled nervously. "It will all be fine."

Ben nodded. "I'm sure it will. I know Sam probably has a lot of willing babysitters, but remember my mom too." He rolled his eyes. "She definitely has a lot of energy and needs something to do."

Jenna tipped her cup and took a sip of coffee. "I appreciate it. That would be great to have her just in case I need someone."

That sat in silence while Jenna wondered why Ben was so interested in Abby and the baby. Really, they barely knew each other. Why would he care? As if he could read her mind, Ben tried to explain.

"Jenna, I'm not sure if you realize it or not but... well, I think about you a lot." He looked down and then back up into her eyes. "I don't want to scare you or push you so please don't worry. There's just something about you."

Jenna tensed. She liked Ben too, but it was too soon. What would people say?

"If there's anything you need, please don't hesitate to call me." Ben took a business card out of his wallet and gave it to Jenna. "Please don't look so scared."

Jenna slowly took the card, looking at it oddly. All of a sudden, she stood up, her cup only half empty. "I appreciate it. I really do, but I'm just not ready."

Jenna turned and walked out of the cafeteria. She knew it was probably all in her head, but it felt like everyone was looking at her, accusing her, and judging her.

Chapter 20

Ben watched Jenna practically run out of the cafeteria. Sighing deeply, he realized he pushed her too fast, too soon. He said he wouldn't, but he couldn't help himself. When their hands touched in the elevator, he took hers before he even knew what he was doing. It felt so right. He got so emotional when he saw Abby and the baby, like they were his own. Ben tried to shake the nervous feeling off. Just like Jenna said, it would all be fine. He would wait as long as it took and hope eventually she would come around.

Ben exited the hospital. The heat outside was blistering. He found his car and turned the air-conditioner on high. As he sat waiting for the car to cool off, he looked to his left. He couldn't believe it, but Jenna was right there next to him, her head leaning against the steering wheel. Eventually she looked up and then right at him, tears running down her face. They stared at each other until finally he got out of his car and got in her passenger side. He didn't ask but pulled her to him and held her. He held her while she cried. He rubbed her back, kissed the top of her head, and said every soothing word he could think of.

He finally heard her murmur into his shirt, "Can you get a napkin out of my glove box?" When he pushed the button to open it, a bunch fell out and they both laughed.

"Do you want one or twenty?"

"A couple will do." She blew her nose and then wiped it. "Thank you."

"I just hope you're not crying because of me."

Jenna shook her head no. "Of course not; it's just been a very emotional time and you're so nice." She looked at his shirt and saw wet splotches on it. "Oh no, you're shirt's all wet." She grabbed another napkin and dabbed at his shirt. "I'm so sorry!"

He stopped her hand and held it, close to his heart. "Stop, Jenna, it's okay."

"But you always look so nice and well dressed." Her bottom lip came out and she started crying again. "And I ruined it."

Ben shook his head. "You didn't ruin anything." He put his finger under her chin. "You could never ruin anything."

Ben knew if he didn't kiss her, he would die right there. He slowly bent his head down giving her time to push him away if that's what she wanted to do. When she didn't, he dove in, and their lips met. He closed his eyes and thought that he must be in heaven. He pulled her closer, touching her hair and rubbing his hands down her back. He sighed when he felt her arms go around his neck. They kissed like he'd never kissed anyone before, feeling like he had finally come home. She was what he had been waiting for his whole life. He wanted to shout for joy until everyone knew how happy he was.

Jenna was the first to pull away. "Wow. That was unexpected."

They were both breathing heavily in the air-conditioned car. He didn't want the moment to end, but he knew it would no matter how hard he tried to hold on to it. He took her hand, bringing it to his lips. "Wow is right."

"Look, Ben, I guess you've figured out that I have a few feelings for you too, but I'm still not ready. I've got so much on my plate right now." Unbelievably, her hand came up and cupped his cheek. "You are an amazing man, and I don't expect you to wait." Ben shook his head and wanted to tell her that he would wait forever, but she stopped him from talking with her finger. "No, Ben, don't say anything. Thank you. Thank you for being there when I really needed you. If it's meant to be, God will let us know, right?"

Ben nodded, because of course she was right.

"I'm here, whenever you need me." He took her in his arms, hugging her because he didn't know when he would be able to touch her again. He spoke into her soft hair. "I'll be waiting, as long as it takes. You promise to let me know if you need anything?" He felt her nod and squeezed her one last time.

He got out of her car and back into his own and prayed to God that it wouldn't be long.

Chapter 21

Jenna was sitting at the kitchen table when Rachel walked in. She had a spoon and a big pot, scraping the remainder of the rice cereal and melted marshmallows that were stuck at the bottom. She had been thinking about Ben and their kiss. She was excited and mortified all at the same time. Rachel sat down at the table.

"Boy, that must taste pretty good. You've got sticky cereal all around your mouth and on your arms too." She took her finger and tried to pry a gob of the sticky mess off of the pot and put it in her mouth. "Yum, why are they so good?" She licked her fingers and then took a napkin, wiping Jenna's face.

"I'm trying to keep busy so that I won't be so overbearing with Abby and the baby."

"Did she say you were overbearing?"

Jenna sighed. "Not in those exact words, but I can tell." Jenna got up and put the pot in the sink and turned the hot tap water on. "I can't help it. She does it all wrong and I'm on pins and needles watching her."

Rachel laughed. "You got any coffee left?"

"I'll make a fresh pot. I could use some too."

While Jenna busied herself with making coffee, Rachel asked, "What does she do wrong?"

Jenna looked toward the door to make sure Abby wasn't eavesdropping. She held up her hand and held up a finger for each point she made.

"One, she tries to feed Sam all the time, even if he so much as grunts. Two, she can't change a diaper to save her life and every time he poops it runs out. Three, she sleeps like the dead and can't hear him during the night. Four, she doesn't support his head good when she holds him, and five, if she says, 'If dad were here' one more time, I'm going to scream." Jenna held up her hands in defeat. "So, I decided to come in here and make something sweet and to heck with it. I got a little carried away, and I'm a whole lot of sticky, but it's been worth it."

"Good for you." Rachel patted Jenna on the shoulder. "Hang in there, sweetie. It will get better."

Jenna rubbed her face with both hands. "It has to."

Rachel laughed again. "How is Sam? Is the diaper rash better?"

Jenna smiled. "He's wonderful. Oh, my goodness, Rachel, he is the sweetest. I could just eat him up! His rash is much better. We've been letting his butt air-dry a little bit more before we put the cream on, and that is really helping. So, what's going on with you? Have you heard anything more from Jason?"

It was Rachel's turn to smile. "Yes. We've been writing back and forth a lot. I think he got his quirky sense of humor from me." Rachel put her hand on her heart. "I'm so proud."

"That's awesome!" Jenna got up and got two cups from the cupboard and set them on the table. "Do you think you'll see him anytime soon?"

"I don't know. I definitely don't want to push him." Jenna handed her the milk and filled up her cup with the steaming coffee. "So, have you heard anything from Ben?" Jenna had told her all about seeing Ben at the hospital and about them kissing in the car.

Jenna sat down and slowly sipped her coffee. "No. I told you I don't have time for that."

"But the kiss...you said it was amazing."

"It was and he is, but can you imagine how people would talk?"

Rachel set her coffee cup down and pointed her finger at Jenna. "Don't you dare worry about what people would say! He's a great guy and you're so lucky. Please don't let him get away because you're worried about what people would say."

Jenna looked down stubbornly. "I can't help it. How was your date, by the way?" Rachel had a blind date, one her neighbor had set up.

Rachel rolled her eyes. "Another stinker." She held her nose for emphasis.

Jenna shook her head. "What was wrong with this guy?"

"Well, for one thing he's a loud sneezer. He about scared the life out of me in the car."

Jenna rubbed her eyebrows. "Really, a loud sneezer? For crying out loud, Rachel, nobody is perfect."

"It wasn't just that. He insisted on opening every dadgum door the whole night. I couldn't even get out of the car until he came around and opened it for me. Made a big deal out of it too, like he was some Romeo." She held up her hands and shook them. "Big whoop!" When Jenna laughed, Rachel said, "Seriously, Jenna, you are so lucky to have a great guy that wants to date you. Believe me, there are a lot of duds out there, so don't let him get away. I know!"

Before Jenna could respond, they heard the baby cry. They both jumped up and ran towards the bedroom to check on him. Abby was sitting in the rocker trying to put the pacifier in his mouth, but he kept spitting it back out.

"I think he's hungry." Abby gave them both a frustrated look. "Would you hold him while I go heat up a bottle?"

Jenna nodded. "Yes, it's almost time anyway. It's been almost three hours, so that's good."

Abby handed the baby to Jenna and then grabbed her phone, heading for the door. "I'll be back in a minute."

Rachel held her hands out. "Give him to me. I need a little Sam lovin'." She sat down in the rocker and tried to rock him. He squirmed and fussed but Rachel kept on until she finally got him to take the pacifier.

"Did you try some new formulas?" The doctor said that Sam probably had a sensitive stomach, so he gave them some different types of formula to try.

Jenna walked around the nursery, straightening up. "Yes. Dairy doesn't seem to be the issue, so we've tried another brand for sensitive stomachs and that seems to be helping a lot." She sat down on the single bed in the room. "We've been sleeping in shifts on this bed."

"Is he wearing the little monitor on his foot that I bought?"

"Oh, yes. Every night. It gives all of his vitals and lets us know how long he sleeps and how often he wakes up. I wish I had one of those when Abby was a baby. I would wake her up all the time fearing she'd stopped breathing."

Rachel nodded towards the crib. "I see the crib hasn't fallen apart yet." It took them almost a whole day, but Jenna and Rachel finally put the crib together themselves. Once it was done, they had a few parts left, but they had no idea where they went.

Jenna laughed. "So far, so good."

Abby walked in with the bottle and Rachel held up her hand for it. Sam sucked as if he was starved to death, and they all laughed. "Mom, do you mind if I go with Katy to grab a burger?"

Jenna shook her head. "No. You go ahead. Sam will be fine with us."

Abby walked over to place a kiss on top of the baby's head. "I'll text you later and let you know when I'm headed home."

Jenna and Rachel watched her practically run out of the room. Rachel grinned and spoke in a baby voice to Sam. "I think your mama needs a little time to herself."

Jenna rolled her eyes. "Yes. I think the newness has worn off a bit and she's ready to get back to it. Isaac is settling in the college life and doesn't have a whole lot of time for his girlfriend and baby. Thank goodness his parents are contributing financially."

"Are they still dating?"

"She says he's become a little distant and doesn't ask much about the baby." Jenna raised her hands. "I'm really not surprised. I know they had good intentions but really, they had no idea what they were getting into. He's in the college life now. I think he probably puts it at the back of his mind."

"Are you okay?"

Jenna smiled fondly at Sam. "Yes. Sometimes he feels like my own baby, and I have to share him with Abby. I think how Craig would have loved him. He would be so proud."

Sam began sucking air, so Rachel took the bottle out of his mouth and held him up, patting his back. "You know I will help all I can too."

Jenna handed Rachel a burp cloth. "Ben said to keep his mother in mind if I need a babysitter. What do you think about that?"

"Really? I think that's a great idea. Go for it."

Sam belched loudly. "Whoa!" Rachel laughed. "You sound like one of my dates!"

Jenna walked to the closet and pulled out the crocheted blanket. "Nancy made this. Isn't it beautiful?"

Rachel exclaimed over the blanket. "Yes. It really is. I can't imagine all the stitches she put in it." Rachel looked thoughtful. "You need to invite Nancy and Ben over so they can see little Sam. You can see how she interacts with him and get a good idea how she is with babies."

Jenna nodded. "You think that would be okay?"

"Of course it will be okay. Why do you worry so much?"

Jenna sighed. "I don't know. I do know that I need to get over it."

Chapter 22

Ben was sitting in the evening rush hour traffic headed home when he got a text from Jenna.

I was wondering if you and your mother would like to come over to see the baby Saturday, about 3:00.

They had been texting occasionally since the baby had been born. The first time she texted him was to get his and his mother's addresses so she could send a thank you note. He had followed up a couple of times to check on her. She responded but didn't say much, so he let it go. Having her invite him and his mother over was a shocker. His mind kept going back to holding her hand in the elevator and later, kissing her in her car. He had never felt so alive. He missed seeing her in church, but Rachel kept him updated. Knowing he would see her soon put a huge smile on his face. He decided to go straight to his mother's so he could ask her.

Nancy was sitting on her porch talking to one of her neighbors when he pulled up. Mrs. Green lived a couple of doors down and Ben had known her for most of his life.

Nancy was surprised to see him. "I wish you had told me you were stopping by. I don't have any dinner prepared; I was just going to eat a sandwich."

Ben had one foot on the sidewalk and one on the front porch step. "I'm not staying long enough for dinner. Hey, Mrs. Green, how's it going?"

"Hey there, Benji, you sure are looking handsome." She actually winked at him, causing Ben to feel just a tad embarrassed. "Your mom and I were just discussing those senior dating websites. What's your opinion on them? I told Nancy to go for it."

Ben looked at Nancy, whose eyes were as round as saucers. Nancy shook her head quickly. "I'm not interested in checking out any dating websites."

Mrs. Green interrupted. "That's not what you just told me. You said..."

"Oh, I was just carrying on." Nancy crossed her arms in aggravation and looked at her friend. "Really, Betty, you know I was just kidding."

Mrs. Green stood up in a huff. "Then why did you ask me what the best websites were, Nancy?" She brushed past Ben as she slowly stepped off the porch. "It was good seeing you again, Benji."

Ben would have laughed at their little tiff if his mom didn't look so aggravated. Instead, he sat down in Mrs. Green's vacated rocking chair. "Mom, it's nothing to be embarrassed about. If you want to check out the websites, it's fine, just be careful and don't give anyone any personal information."

"I know. I'm not an idiot." Her rocker was rocking a little faster than usual, which showed her agitation. "Betty is just so crass. She'll say anything and tell everyone your business." Ben almost interrupted his mother to say he knew all about that, but Nancy continued, "I knew better than to tell her anything. One time she told the whole neighborhood that I had breast cancer. I mentioned that I had a lump, which turned out to be just a cyst, and then all my neighbors were sending me cards and calling with condolences. I was never so embarrassed in all my life."

Ben remembered that time. His mother just knew she had cancer and was surprised when it turned out to be a cyst, which was easily drained. "I'm sure she means well."

"Did I tell anyone that her husband was having an affair with the widow Ruth Carter 20 years ago? No. I knew there was some hanky panky going on, but I kept my mouth shut. The man was making every excuse in the world to go to Ruth's house. It didn't take a rocket scientist to figure it out." Ben kept quiet, knowing that his mom was going to vent it out no matter what he said. "And another thing... Betty Green had a boob lift. Can you believe that? At her age! Why, it's the silliest thing I ever heard. And I never told a soul." Nancy took a deep breath. "I'll never tell her anything else, as long as I live. That's the gospel truth."

Ben didn't figure there was any gospel in it, but he decided to say what he had come for to get her off her rant.

"Would you like to go see Abby's baby Saturday?"

"Jenna's Abby?"

Ben nodded. "Yes, about three. I'll take you to lunch first and we'll make a day of it."

"Of course, that sounds wonderful!"

They rocked in silence until Ben said, "I told her that you may be interested in keeping the baby in an emergency. I hope that's okay. With Jenna working and Abby going to school, they need some people they can count on.

"There is one thing I need to tell you." His mom looked perplexed, but Ben soldiered on. "The baby is of mixed race. His father is black. I wanted to let you know so that you would be prepared and not stare or anything."

Nancy's rocker stopped. "Oh, for goodness sake, Benji. I'm not going to do or say anything to embarrass you." She began rocking again and smiled. "Vera's daughter is married to a black man and they have five children. Why, I've never seen any cuter babies. What about Jenna's mother?"

"I'm sure she will be on standby as well. I just thought that it would be something you would love."

"Oh yes. I can't wait to hold the baby." Nancy looked thoughtful. "So, you've been talking to Jenna?"

Ben was staring at a spider web on the porch railing, strategically placed to catch bugs flying towards the porch light. He considered carefully what information he wanted to share with his mom. Finally, he said, "Yes. After I dropped off the baby blanket and gifts, we've texted a little."

"You like her, don't you?"

Ben nodded. "Yes. I do like her, a lot, but she's not ready for anything right now, so I don't know if anything will ever come of it."

He didn't mention the kiss that rocked his whole world and how every time he thought of it his heart would race. He didn't mention the fact that he dreamed of her almost every night, and on the nights he didn't dream of her, he woke up disappointed and bummed. He also didn't mention the fact that he probably had her dead husband's heart beating in his own body. His mom might get too excited and blab it to Betty Green, and then the whole neighborhood would know.

Nancy smiled and patted her son's hand. "She seems like a very sweet girl."

Ben knew she was sweet. She tasted sweeter than anything he could have imagined. Before his thoughts were out of control, Ben stood up. "Well, I have a couple of errands to run before I get home. I've got a big deadline at work tomorrow, so I need to get a good night's rest."

Nancy stood up too. "Call me and let me know what time you're picking me up for lunch Saturday. I love you."

"I love you, too, Mom."

Chapter 23

Jenna didn't know why she was so nervous. It was almost as if having Ben and his mother come to her house was momentous. She didn't want to encourage Ben, but she also didn't want him to think she didn't care. She thought about him all the time, especially their kiss. She alternated between feeling guilty, as if she was cheating on Craig, and also of feeling excited and wanting to kiss him again. She knew she shouldn't worry about what people would say. Rachel was right. But sometimes she would think about Craig, and everything would come crashing down again. It would take her awhile to crawl back out of her funk. Thankfully, those times were coming less often, but it still hurt. It still hurt knowing she would never see her soul mate again. Ben would never be her soul mate. Nobody could ever take Craig's place.

Jenna was wrapping the vacuum cleaner cord up when she heard her mother knock and then walk in the kitchen door. She glanced at the baby monitor to make sure Sam was still asleep and then walked in to greet her mom.

Elizabeth was carrying a big box of diapers.

"Aw, thanks, Mom, I forgot how many diapers a baby can go through."

"I found these on sale." She placed the box on the kitchen table and sat down. "Can I do anything before your company comes?" Jenna had told her about Ben and Nancy coming to see the baby and that she thought it would be nice if her mom came as well. Of course, Elizabeth grilled her on why they were coming. Jenna told her that Nancy was from her church and was a potential babysitter.

They both heard Sam cry out on the baby monitor. Jenna said, "Can you get Sam up for me and check his diaper? I'm sure it needs changing. I'll get his bottle ready and then you can feed him."

"Of course." As she walked out of the kitchen she said, "Where's Abby?"

"Isaac is in this weekend. They left a little bit ago. She'll be back soon."

Jenna grabbed a prepared bottle out of the refrigerator and stuck it in the warmer. While she waited, she took some cookies she had made earlier and placed them on a plate. Once that was done, she ground some coffee, poured the water in the reservoir, and pushed the 'on' button. By the time she was done with that, the bottle was ready. After checking to make sure it wasn't too hot, she took it to Sam's room. Elizabeth was rocking and cooing to Sam. "You're such a good baby, yes you are! Nana loves you!"

Jenna handed the bottle to her mom and then sat on the small bed. "We've been giving him a little less milk but more often. It seems to be helping him spit up less."

"Looks like he's getting plenty." Elizabeth rocked in the glider as she gave Sam his bottle, smiling at him. "I swear he grows more every time I see him. If he gets too hungry, put a little baby cereal in his milk. That will fill his little tummy."

"The doctors discourage giving them anything besides milk for the first couple of months."

Elizabeth guffawed. "It never hurt you and it never hurt Abby. Doctors change their minds one year to the next. First, they said to put them on their stomach, then no, put them on their side, and then, put them on their back. Good grief, I wish they'd make up their minds." Elizabeth looked at the crib. "And then they tell you to not put pads or blankets in their cribs. I bet you that the first time he rolls into the rail and hits his head, you'll wish you had a pad or two."

"The doctors know more than us. I don't want Sam to be that one statistic."

"I bet they say one thing and do another, you follow?"

Jenna decided she was in no mood to argue or contradict her mother.

"Our first workday is Wednesday. I'm taking Sam to the daycare at church Monday for about three hours just to see how he does. I'll put you on the emergency contact list, but they may need you to come in at some point so they can get a copy of your driver's license."

Sam finished his bottle, so Elizabeth held him up to pat his back. "If you ask me, you seem more like the mom than Abby does."

Jenna was tired of giving excuses for Abby. She knew that Abby was guilty of letting Jenna carry most of the responsibilities, but Jenna knew she was guilty as well for allowing it. "I know, Mom but it is what it is." Jenna got up and put the dirty diaper in the pail and got a clean outfit out of the closet. "She thought she was ready, but it's obvious to her and everyone else that she's not." Jenna sighed. "She even said she feels more like Sam's sister than his mother." Even that was a shock to Jenna.

"You mark my words, Jenna, if you don't put your foot down, you're going to be raising this baby. Is that what you want?"

Jenna didn't argue because deep down she knew her mom was right this time, but Sam would never have to worry as long as Jenna was alive. She would always be there for him.

Chapter 24

B en's heart skipped a beat when Jenna opened the door and smiled. She was holding Sam who squinted when the sun hit his face. Nancy exclaimed over the baby while Jenna invited them in. They were led into the living room where Jenna's mother was sitting on one of the chairs. They were all introduced and then Jenna asked Nancy if she would like to hold him.

"Oh, my goodness, yes!" She sat down on one end of the couch and held out her hands. "What a darling little boy you are!" Sam yawned and made some funny faces. Ben watched Jenna smile at Sam like he had won the spelling bee.

Ben couldn't believe how much he had grown in such a short time. "He doesn't even look like the same baby." He sat down next to his mom and touched Sam's hand. Sam's fingers grasped Ben's finger and he was hooked. Ben couldn't even begin to describe the feeling of seeing this little boy. He had been around children before but never felt any kind of connection. It was all he could do to give his mom her turn before he took the baby himself.

While he looked in awe at Sam, Jenna's mother asked him if he also went to their same church. Ben nodded. "Yes, for a few months now."

Nancy put Sam up against her shoulder and patted. "Benji's been going with me since this past spring. At first, I had to drag him but now he looks forward to it. What church do you go to?"

"I've been going to the same church for a few years now. It's the Presbyterian church on Maple." Elizabeth shook her head. "Our attendance has been slowly declining for the past few years, but they're pretty set in their ways and aren't a fan of change. We don't have a lot of young members."

While Elizabeth informed them of ways that she thought her church could increase their attendance, Ben watched Jenna get up and get a plate of cookies off the bar that separated the kitchen from the living room. After placing the plate on the coffee table, she waited for her mom to stop talking and then asked if anyone wanted coffee or a cold drink. Once she got everyone's orders, she headed towards the kitchen. Ben got up and followed her.

"Can I help you?"

Jenna pointed towards the refrigerator. "You can get the half and half out for me."

Ben opened the door and glanced inside until he finally located the milk. He took it out and set it on the counter, standing next to Jenna. Her dark hair was pulled back in a ponytail and she had a blue cotton summer dress that came just above her knee. "I'll fix mine and my mother's."

Jenna nodded and poured coffee in four mugs. "Thanks. How have you been?" Her hand shook slightly as if she was nervous.

Pouring milk into one cup, Ben said, "Busy at work. It's really picked up this summer, how about you?"

Jenna grimaced. "I have to go back to work Wednesday. I dread it."

Ben would give anything to pull her into his arms and console her. "Are you worried about Sam?"

Jenna nodded. "Yeah, I don't want to leave him."

Ben couldn't stop himself from touching Jenna's ponytail and then patting her back softly. "I'm sorry." Jenna looked at him and he melted. They didn't speak with their mouths, but their eyes spoke volumes. The spell was finally broken when Elizabeth walked up to the bar. They jumped apart like they had been kissing instead of just gazing into each other's eyes.

"Can I help carry the cups?" Jenna's mother was looking at them oddly. "Did I interrupt anything?"

Jenna slid a cup towards her mother. "Of course not, Ben was just telling me how much Nancy loves babies."

As they all walked back towards the living room, Ben sat down beside his mom again. "Do you mind if I hold him now?" Nancy handed him the baby reluctantly. "I think he's getting sleepy."

Ben looked down at Sam. Sam yawned again and stretched his arms. "He sure is handsome." Ben brought him up to his face. "And he smells so good." Ben barely listened to the conversation around him while he cuddled a contented Sam. Eventually the baby fell asleep. Ben looked at Jenna. "Can I just hold him, or do you want to put him down?"

"I know he feels like heaven, but I guess we better put him down. He can get pretty cranky if he doesn't sleep well." Jenna stood up and headed toward the bedrooms. "His bedroom is this way."

Ben got up and followed Jenna. The walls in the nursery were pale blue and the furniture was all white. Jenna closed the shades and turned on some white noise and motioned for Ben to lay the baby down. She whispered, "Lay him down on his back."

Ben laid him down gently and expected him to wake up, but Sam closed his eyes as soon as Jenna placed a pacifier in his mouth. They stood beside each other looking down at the baby, both smiling. Ben whispered, "I've missed you."

At first Ben didn't think Jenna heard him but she turned towards him and placed her hands around his waist, hugging him. "I've missed you too." He pulled her closer and kissed the top of her head. Too quickly she stepped back and walked towards the door, and he had no choice but to follow.

Chapter 25

"What's going on between you and Ben?"

Jenna sighed. She wondered how long it would take her mom to ask that question. "Nothing." She busied herself in the kitchen putting the remaining cookies in a storage bag.

"Nothing, my foot. I'm not blind."

Jenna stopped what she was doing and looked at her mom. "Would it be so awful if there was?"

Elizabeth stared back at her daughter. "It would be too soon, and you have no business getting involved with anyone right now. I made sure you were my first priority after your father died and you need to do the same with Abby and Sam." Jenna turned to load the coffee cups in the dishwasher, but Elizabeth stopped her. "Please tell me you're not involved with another man. It's not even been a year yet, Jenna."

Jenna threw the towel down on the counter that had been draped across her shoulder. "Of course I'm not involved! Do you think I've had time to run around and have a boyfriend in the last few months? For goodness sakes, Mom, give me a break."

Elizabeth looked knowingly. "Well, as I said, I'm not blind and I can see something is going on." She took her pocketbook off the wall hook and walked towards the door. "I would hate to hear people talking about you behind your back saying Craig hasn't even been in the grave a year and you're already carrying on, you follow?" Cluck Cluck.

Jenna counted to 10 after her mom left and then sat down and cried. She was crying when Abby came in the front of the house, slamming the door behind her. Jenna jumped up, wiped her eyes, and followed Abby to her room. "What in the world is going on?"

Abby threw herself down on the bed, crying in her pillow and mumbled, "Isaac and I broke up."

Jenna sat down on the bed beside her. "Oh, honey, I'm so sorry."

Abby rolled over and draped her hand on top of her face. "He's such a jerk. He said he needs his space and more time to concentrate on school." When Jenna didn't say anything, Abby continued ranting. "That is such a load of bull. Katy heard a rumor that he's been hanging around a girl at school a lot, and they're probably already dating."

Abby began crying again so Jenna got up and got some tissues. "Abby, please don't cry." Jenna took a tissue and dabbed her daughter's eyes.

Abby grabbed another tissue and blew her nose loudly. "He didn't even want to see Sam! His own baby!"

Jenna wasn't surprised and knew in her heart that this was coming, but it still hurt to see her daughter so upset. Jenna pulled Abby into her arms and comforted her the only way she knew how, by loving her unconditionally and totally. Eventually Abby calmed down and then they heard Sam crying. Jenna brought him to Abby and laid him in her arms. "I'll go warm up his bottle. Be right back."

When she came back, it warmed Jenna's heart to see Abby cradling Sam and hushing his cries. Abby took the bottle and placed it in Sam's mouth, and he sucked hungrily. Jenna watched and couldn't help but be thankful. She knew things would get better, but Abby was young and lived in the moment. She couldn't think about the past and what brought her here, and she had no vision of the future. She was surprised when Abby said, "Mom, why would God take Daddy and let that awful man who killed him live?"

Jenna closed her eyes and thought about the answer. She had thought that so many times as well. Why would God let that happen? Jenna would get mad when she would hear people say that *everything happens for a reason*. Personally, she thought that was the most hurtful thing to say to someone who had lost a loved one. What could possibly be the reason? But she understood now, after much prayer and soul searching. "Honey, God does not sit in heaven guiding everyone around like a puppet. He lets us make our own choices, and sometimes those choices are good and sometimes they're bad. Good or bad, those choices affect other people."

Abby looked thoughtful. "But why wouldn't God help us make good choices so this earth would be a better place? Life would be so much better and we would all be happy."

Jenna took Abby's free hand. "How would you feel if your father and I had made every choice for you? What if we made you thank us and revere us and made you say that you loved us? Do you think we would be proud of you for doing what we made you do? Do you think saying *I love you* would mean as much? When I see you doing well I am so proud of you, because you made those choices. When you say *I love you*, I know you say it because you mean it and not because I made you."

"But how can you make the right choices all the time, and even if you did, when someone else screws up, you still have to pay for their mistakes, like Daddy?"

"That's why it's so important for you to accept Jesus into your heart, sweetie. Once you do, the Holy Spirit is within you all the time, helping you and guiding you. When you're hurt, you pray and let God carry you through because you can't do it by yourself. Sometimes we still ignore what we know is right because we're all sinners, but God gives us that choice. Can you imagine how proud He is when we do well and we do what's right, because that was our choice and not because He made us. Does that make sense?"

Abby nodded. "Yeah, it makes sense. I think I get it." She was silent for a moment and then said, "Could you ever forgive that man who killed Daddy because I don't think I ever could." She shook her head adamantly.

Jenna sighed. "It's been something I've thought about a lot, Abby. At first, no, I had a deep hatred for him, but it was killing me inside. I finally had to let it go and I'm so glad I did. If I saw him today and he asked for my forgiveness, I would give it to him. Nothing we do is unforgivable as long as we are sorry and ask God to forgive us. If God forgives, don't you think He wants us to forgive as well?"

"Yeah, probably." Abby picked Sam up and cuddled him, patting his little behind. "Thank you, mom." She smiled at Sam and then at Jenna. "I do love you, so much. I don't know what I would have done if you hadn't been there for me or had been like Rachel's parents."

Abby and Jenna both started crying again. "I love you, too, Abby, always, and your daddy is watching you from heaven. I know he's so proud of you."

Chapter 26

"Jenna's mother is something else, don't ya think?" Nancy had been talking non-stop since they left Jenna's house. At first it was all about the baby, but then she started in on Elizabeth. She shook her head in admonishment. "It was all I could do to keep her from going into the bedroom when you and Jenna were putting little Sam down. I talked non-stop asking her every question I could think to ask."

Ben grinned just imagining his mom talking even more than usual.

"I appreciate it, but nothing happened." Ben thought of Jenna hugging him and kept that memory in his heart. He knew it was hard for Jenna, that she was fighting her feelings for him. She did have feelings for him, though, and that warmed him all over.

"I have a feeling that she will not take kindly to her daughter dating again. She made a point in telling me that she stayed true to Jenna's father all these years and you could tell she was very proud of that fact." She pointed ahead. "Can you stop at the grocery store up ahead? I need to grab some milk and bread."

Ben nodded and turned into the parking lot. Once he was parked, he said, "I'll keep the car running while you shop. Take your time." He immediately got out his phone and texted Jenna.

Thanks for letting us come over and see Sam today. My mom can't stop talking about how cute he is. Hope to see you soon. Are you coming to church tomorrow?

He put the phone on the dash and then picked it up again to check his mail. After opening each one and responding accordingly, he put it back down. He knew she was probably busy, but he was hoping for a response. He finally heard the text notification, but it wasn't from Jenna, it was from Rachel.

Jenna told me that you and your mother were coming by today. How'd it go? Did you get to meet Elizabeth? She's a peach.

Ben smiled. She must know all about Elizabeth.

Had a great visit and yes, Elizabeth is a real peach. LOL. Mom loved Sam and can't stop talking about him.

Rachel's response was immediate.

Jenna told me about the kiss. Before you get any closer, you need to tell her the truth about your heart.

Ben's stomach dropped. Maybe he should go ahead and tell her, but she was so skittish, like a scared animal. That may be all it would take to make her run forever.

I promise to tell her soon.

Ben put his phone down and tried to imagine how he would tell her. He was so deep in thought that he was startled when Nancy opened the car door and sat down.

"Sorry it took so long. I ran into Larry. We got to talking and he asked me to dinner tonight." She put her seatbelt on and then got some hand sanitizer out of her purse. "I really don't care about going but I sort of felt sorry for him. I have been avoiding him if you want to know the truth. He's nice and all but he has a bad habit of talking about his dead wife. I don't mind him talking about her some but really, just about every subject that comes up he's got a story to tell about her. Apparently, she was the best cook ever and made all her own clothes. I appreciate the fact that he admired her, but if you're with another lady you need to zip it."

Ben was hardly listening to a word his mother was saying. He was thinking about what Rachel said. He decided to talk to his mother about it and see what she said. Once they were home and her milk and bread put away, Ben was waiting for his mom to draw a breath so he could ask her. Finally, he said, "Mom, let's go sit down. There's something I need to talk to you about."

"Sounds serious." Nancy led the way into the living room and sat down in her favorite chair. "Okay, let's hear it."

Ben drew a deep breath. "There's something you need to know about Jenna." He paused and wondered if he was making a big mistake by telling his mother, but against his better judgment, he plundered on. "You know that Jenna's husband died in a car accident, right?"

"Yes. He was hit by a drunk driver last fall."

Ben leaned forward in his seat, resting his elbows on his knees, his hands clasped together under his chin. "He was brain dead but kept alive long enough so that some of his organs could be donated." He looked at his mother and saw the truth dawn in her eyes. He watched her fist go to her mouth in shock.

Ben nodded. "I think I received Craig's heart, Mom."

"Oh, my goodness, does Jenna know?"

Ben shook his head. "No, and therein lies the crutch."

"How long have you known?"

"A few weeks, remember when Rachel called?"

Nancy looked at him in reproach. "I knew it was more than about a job!"

Looking sheepishly, Ben affirmed her statement. "Yes, it was, a lot more. I actually guessed it before and then you mentioned to her that day after church about my transplant and she guessed it. I'm really just assuming it's true, but it's just too much of a coincidence not to be."

"So, are you afraid to tell Jenna?"

"Yes, she's so conflicted right now. You can see the pressure her mother puts on her and then everything with Abby and the baby. She's fighting it and I don't want to..." Ben just couldn't put it into words.

"You don't want to scare her any more than she already is." When Ben nodded, she continued, "But why would that scare her, Benji? I would think that would make her feel even closer to you."

"But what if it doesn't, Mom? What if she thinks that Craig had to die so that I could live?" He couldn't help the tears that filled his eyes. Saying it out loud scared him to death. What if she really did feel that way? What if she found out and hated him for it?

Nancy got up and sat down beside Ben on the couch, putting her arm around his shoulders. "Oh, honey, how could she hate you? Anyone with eyeballs in their head can see she cares for you, even when she's trying to hide it."

Ben sniffed. "But if I told her the truth, that could change."

Nancy patted his knee like a child. "Listen, Benji, have you prayed about it?"

"I've tried. It just sounds so juvenile." Ben's mouth was dry, and he almost choked trying to get the words out. "God already gave me another chance at life. Now I'm asking for the girl who was married to the guy who gave me his heart? Sounds a little selfish if you ask me."

Nancy shook her head. "Absolutely not; nothing is too big or too small for God. He listens to every prayer and wants to hear from you, even about the most trivial things. He will not only answer your prayer to His will, but he will also help you if the answer is not what you want or expect. Either way, you can't go wrong by seeking his guidance."

Ben took a deep breath. "I know you're right." He rubbed his face and eyes. He placed his hands on his legs and rubbed up and down. He needed to get home and do some soul searching. "I need to get home." He stood up and walked towards the door. "Have a great time with Larry tonight."

Nancy stood up too. "I don't have to go if you need to talk more."

Ben opened the door and then turned and looked at his mom. "You don't know how much I appreciate you, for always being there for me." He pulled her in a big hug and kissed her cheek. "I love you."

Nancy put her arms around her son and squeezed. "Not as much as I love you."

Later that evening, Ben did something he hadn't done in a long time. He got on his knees and poured his heart out to God. His mother was right. It was exactly what he needed.

Chapter 27

Jenna stood in the bathroom, under the glare of the fluorescent lights. She had dark circles under her eyes and her hair was up in a clip, with stray hairs stuck out at every angle. She forgot what it was like to get a good night of uninterrupted sleep. Even between the two of them, Jenna and Abby still struggled. At least with them being on summer break, they could catch a short nap here and there during the day. This next week would be a test for both of them. She washed her face, brushed her teeth, and grabbed her nightgown hanging on a hook on the back of the bathroom door. Once she was in the bed, she took off her socks and then rubbed her dry feet with lotion and then put her socks back on. She went to grab her phone from the nightstand but realized she had left it in the kitchen. She tiptoed down the hallway, glancing in Abby's room as she did. She could see her daughter scrolling on her phone intently. Once Jenna had her own phone, she walked back to her bedroom and got under the covers. She had some text messages, several from Rachel and one from Ben. She looked at Rachel's first.

How'd it go today?

Was Elizabeth nice? You follow?

Just got home from my date with Mr. Wrong. He had three alcoholic drinks before we even got to the main course and was slurring his words by dessert. I called an Uber.

I'm going to bed but text me no matter how late you get this message and let me know you're okay.

Jenna saw that it hadn't been long since Rachel had sent the last text message. She responded.

Things went well, I think. Elizabeth was Elizabeth. I'll tell you about that tomorrow. Nancy was so sweet and Ben was so cute holding Sam. Abby and Isaac broke up and she was pretty upset but I think everything is okay now. We'll be at church tomorrow so I'll see you there.

She opened up Ben's message and smiled and kept smiling while she typed a reply.

Thanks for coming, Ben. We'll definitely be at church tomorrow so I'll see you in the morning. I was wondering if you'd like to come over tomorrow evening and have some pizza or something with us? Jenna looked at the message and wondered if it was a bad idea to ask him over. She thought of what her mom would say and stubbornly pushed send before she could change her mind. He replied almost instantly.

I would love that. Just let me know what time.

* * *

Jenna was second guessing herself by Sunday afternoon. She couldn't believe that she actually invited Ben over, by himself. She still hadn't told Abby. Even Rachel was surprised but as usual, supportive in her own quirky way. "Don't do anything I wouldn't do, which is not much, so don't get excited."

Jenna laughed. "He's just a friend. There will be no hanky panky, trust me."

Rachel rolled her eyes. "I can practically see the sparks when you two look at each other."

Jenna tried not to smile but failed miserably. "I can't help it. He's just so cute!" She waved her hand in front of her face. "Did you hear him singing in church? He has the best voice."

"Are you kidding? I couldn't hear anyone over Vera. She was practically shouting, 'There's power in the blood,' until my ears started ringing." When Jenna laughed, Rachel giggled too. "Have you ever noticed how close she gets when she talks to you? I'm trying to back up being mindful of my breath and all, and she's getting close enough to count the whiskers on my upper lip."

"You don't have any whiskers!"

"Well, if I did, she could surely count them."

Jenna did some last-minute straightening up in the living room while Sam lay on a baby mat looking up at the baby toys on the attached mobile. He was cooing happily, kicking his legs. Abby walked in and sat down on the couch. "What's for dinner?"

"I'm going to order a pizza in a little bit." Jenna picked up a blanket that was wadded up at the end of the couch, folded it, and draped it over the sofa. "By the way, Ben is coming over to have dinner with us."

Abby had been slumped on the couch, but she sat up and looked at her mom. "Ben? Again?"

Jenna walked into the kitchen and got out some paper plates and placed them on the bar. "Yes. We're just friends but he's really nice and, well, I just thought it would be nice to invite him." Jenna tried to act like it was nothing, but inside she was a nervous wreck. When Abby didn't say anything else, she walked to the opening above the bar and looked at her daughter. "That's okay, isn't it? It's not a big deal."

Abby, being Abby, had her face scrunched up, looking disgusted. "I just think it's weird, but whatever."

Jenna thought, *yeah, whatever*. She turned and began drying the few dishes that were in the dish drainer and put them away. She heard the doorbell ring and walked towards the living room. Abby was standing at the opened door, her hand on her hip. Ben was smiling, but after seeing Abby's definite attitude, his smile fell just a little, causing Jenna to try and pull back her errant daughter. "Hey, Ben, come on in." As Ben walked into the room, Jenna warned her daughter silently with a reproving look. In response, Abby defiantly tossed her head and then marched sassily into her bedroom without a word.

Jenna motioned for Ben to sit down but instead he got on the floor next to Sam. "How's the little guy today? Mom was so jealous when she found out I was coming to see him."

Jenna got down on the floor on the other side of Sam. "He's perfect. He did great in the nursery today at church. I thought I would order pizza in a little bit. That okay?"

Before he answered, Sam sneezed. Jenna said, "Wait for it, he always sneezes three times."

Sam sneezed two more times and Ben laughed. "That's the sweetest little sneeze I've ever heard. I sound like a freight train compared to him."

It was Jenna's turn to laugh. She thought about Rachel's date with the loud sneezer. Chip walked into the room and sat down next to Jenna. Jenna stroked Chip's head. "I hope Sam's not allergic to cats." She picked Chip up and held him towards Ben. "You want a cat? He's really sweet."

Ben sat up and took Chip from her and put him in his lap, petting him. "I love cats. I've been thinking of getting one of my own. My ex-wife wouldn't let me have one."

Jenna watched Ben pet Chip who looked like he was in heaven. "Chip usually never comes out for company. I'm surprised he's letting you even pet him." Sam fussed a little so Jenna picked him up and propped him up in her lap. "So, you've been married? What happened, if you don't mind my asking?"

Ben shook his head. "Not at all, we were only married about five years. She was younger than me." Ben was quiet for a moment and then put Chip down, who began licking his paws. "I got sick a while back, and she left me. She said it hurt her too much to see me suffering."

Jenna looked confused. "She left you because you were sick? Did she not understand the 'in sickness and in health' part of the marriage ceremony?"

Ben shrugged. "No, that didn't seem to resonate with her. It hurt at the time, but I soon realized that it was the best thing that could have happened."

Jenna raised her eyebrows. "That just blows my mind. Wow. You said you were sick. What happened?"

Ben looked at Jenna as if he wasn't sure he wanted to tell her what was wrong. She felt embarrassed that she asked because maybe it was something that he didn't want to share. Jenna was getting ready to stop him from answering but Ben beat her to the punch. "I had a bad heart, just like my dad."

Jenna reached her hand out towards Ben. "I'm so sorry."

Ben took her hand and held it. "It's fine."

Jenna nodded. "Yes. You look so healthy now. You said you had a bad heart. Is everything okay now?"

Ben dropped Jenna's hand and stood up. "Yeah. Everything is great now. Do you have any water?"

Jenna nodded. "Yes. There's some bottled water in the fridge. Go ahead and grab one." Sam was getting fussier, so she got up with him and followed Ben into the kitchen. "Can you grab Sam's bottle for me?" Ben took the bottle out and handed it to Jenna. She put it in the warmer and pressed the 'on' button. "It just takes a couple of minutes. Let me feed him and put him down and then we'll order a pizza."

Ben held his hand out towards Sam. "Can I feed him?"

Jenna smiled. "Of course, go ahead and take him to the nursery and you can rock him in the glider while you feed him. I'll be there in a minute. If he gets too fussy before I bring the bottle, just stick a pacifier in his mouth. There's a bunch of clean ones on the nightstand."

Jenna watched Ben walk towards the bedrooms and wondered how in the world a wife could leave her husband when he was sick. She shook her head. Surely that wasn't the only reason their marriage ended. That was just crazy; nobody could be that callous.

Once the bottle was ready, Jenna took it to the nursery and handed it to Ben. She readied the room while Ben fed Sam. When she was done, she sat down and watched them. Ben was a natural and she could tell that Sam felt very comfortable with him. Once Sam was done with the bottle, his eyes were already closed. He never even woke up when Ben laid him down. They tiptoed out of the room and Jenna closed the door quietly. Once they were in the living room, Jenna turned on the baby monitor. "What kind of pizza do you like?"

Ben sat down on the couch. "I like anything."

Jenna nodded and then went into the kitchen to place the order. As soon as she got off the phone, she came back and sat down next to Ben. He was very quiet, and she could sense a change in him. She stuck her finger in her mouth nervously and nibbled on her nail. "If you don't want to talk about it, Ben, that's fine."

Ben closed his eyes and then looked at Jenna intently. "No, we need to talk about it."

Jenna was baffled. "Why do we need to talk about it?"

It was then that Ben gave her the surprise of her life. "I had a heart transplant."

Chapter 28

Ben watched Jenna's eyes grow round in surprise. "You...you had a heart transplant?"

Ben nodded.

"When? A long time ago?" Jenna's hand was placed over her mouth.

Ben took her other hand and looked at it instead of Jenna's face. He wasn't sure if he could stand it if Jenna looked repulsed when she found out. "When Craig died."

Jenna automatically jerked her hand back and gasped. "You...you... oh my...you have Craig's heart?"

Ben could barely hear her, but he nodded. "I don't know for sure, but it looks pretty likely."

Jenna stood up and began pacing around the living room. "This is unbelievable." She stopped walking. "How long have you known?"

Ben knew he was likely to lose her before he even had her. It was just too much for Jenna. He had fallen hard too. He loved her but it wasn't enough. This would always be between them.

"Remember when we met in the coffee shop that day? You told me how Craig died, and, on a whim, I googled it. I knew his organs were donated and I knew the date he died."

Jenna hugged her arms close and hung her head and then jerked it back up again. "Why didn't *you* tell me?"

Ben sighed. He would give anything to take the pain away he saw in Jenna's eyes. "I don't know. I was scared. Rachel told me..."

Jenna stopped him. "Wait! Rachel knew?"

Ben nodded. "I told her not to say anything yet until I was able to tell you."

Jenna shook her head. "Rachel knew the whole time and I'm just oblivious." Jenna pointed a finger at the door. "I really think you need to leave now. I can't even process this right now. I'm sorry but this will never work."

Ben knew it. It was just like he pictured it, only worse. He walked towards the door. He turned back before he opened it. "I'm sorry, Jenna." When Jenna didn't respond, he left and quietly closed the door behind him.

Ben had to pull over before he even got home. He sobbed like he did when he was a child and his cat died. When he finally was able to calm down, he drove home and walked into his empty, barren condo. It still looked as dull and dismal as the first day he moved in. He had every intention of fixing it up and making it more of a home, but he just never got around to it. He put his keys on the kitchen counter and then grabbed a bottle of water out of the fridge. He sat down on the couch in the darkened living room. Pretty soon it would be completely dark, but he didn't care. He picked up his phone and then threw it back down again. Eventually, his phone started ringing. First it was his mother. He thought about letting it go to voicemail, but he didn't want to worry her.

"Hey, Mom."

"Hey, Benji, how'd it go tonight?"

"Not too good."

"Oh, honey, I'm so sorry. I take it you told her."

"Yeah, I did what you said. I prayed about it and knew the longer I waited the worse it would be, but I don't see how it could be any worse."

"Just give it time."

Ben knew she was only trying to help but he just couldn't pretend that everything would be okay. "Look, I'm real tired. I'm going to bed. I'll call you tomorrow."

The phone rang not long after he hung up with his mother. It was Rachel.

"Ben? Is everything okay with Jenna?"

"No."

"I knew something was going on. She wouldn't answer my texts or my calls. I texted Abby and she said you had left hours ago."

"She knows and she knows you know."

There was a silence and then Rachel said, "Hmm. Well, just let her be for a bit. She'll come around."

"I wouldn't be so sure. She's really mad and hurt."

"Listen, Ben, I've known Jenna a long time. She's my best friend and she's been with me during some of the darkest days of my life. I love her dearly and I would do anything for her, but she can be a bit dramatic sometimes. Who do you think Abby takes it after? Anyway, once she has time to think about it, she'll get over the part about being the last to know. That's really all she's mad about."

Ben voiced his biggest fear. "But what if she's mad because I lived and Craig didn't?"

Rachel replied. "Oh, Ben, is that what you're worried about?"

Ben's silence must have affirmed her question.

"Ben, listen to me. I don't know if it's meant for you and Jenna to be together. I do know that she really likes you. Don't give up on her, but do give her time."

"I'll try. I mean I'll try and give her time and I won't give up on her."

"Good. Now get some sleep and we'll both pray that she'll come around sooner than later. Okay?"

Ben smiled and felt better for the first time since he told Jenna about his heart. "Thanks, Rachel. I really appreciate it."

Ben decided that he would take Rachel's advice. He got ready for bed and lay down. He thought about Sam and how good it felt to hold him. He wanted a child of his own. He had a checkup the following week. Maybe he would ask the doctor if he would be able to adopt. He wasn't sure about the laws and conditions, but it had to be a possibility. He fell asleep thinking about children and how happy his mom would be to have a grandchild.

Chapter 29

Jenna was still mad. She felt so betrayed by Ben and by Rachel. How could they not tell her and leave her in the dark about something so important? Ben should have told her the moment he realized it.

She had dropped Sam off at the daycare and then came straight to work. Abby was at home but going to pick him up about noon. It was very hard to let Abby do it on her own, but Jenna knew she had to let her. Jenna felt herself wanting to control every aspect of Sam's life, but he wasn't her baby, even though she felt like he was more her baby than Abby's. She unlocked the media center door and turned her computer on to let it warm up. The teachers would all be back today as well, and they would want to use the laminator, which was located in the media center workroom. She turned it on and made sure it had plenty of film.

She got to work decorating all of the bulletin boards because the next day they had a faculty meeting that was mandatory and would probably last most of the workday. She had researched and designed the boards during the summer, so it didn't take her long to finish. She had boxes of books to prepare for the shelves and magazines to sort through that had piled up over the summer. Before she knew it, the day was gone, and it was time to go home. Abby had called earlier to let her know that she and Sam had made it home, and the daycare workers said Sam did great. Jenna was a little surprised that Rachel never came by to see her at work, not that she would have much to say to her.

Once she saw Sam, she smiled for the first time since she had woken up that morning. She couldn't believe how much she had missed him. She cuddled and played with him until he got fussy and hungry. After he went to sleep, instead of putting him down, she rocked him. Abby came in and whispered, "Can we have tacos for dinner? I'll go get them."

Jenna nodded and spoke softly. "There's a 20 in the side pocket of my purse."

Abby left and then came back. "Found it. You want three hard shell tacos, like usual?"

"Yes. Could you get me one of those dessert thingies?"

While Abby was gone, Jenna placed Sam in his crib. She had some laundry to do so she started a load and then went to prepare Sam's bottles for the night and following day. Abby eventually came back with the food and sat down at the kitchen table. Jenna joined her and after eating in silence for a few minutes, Abby said, "Mom, what happened with Ben the other night?"

Jenna wiped her mouth and took a drink of her soda. At first, she didn't want to tell Abby about Ben but then decided she would tell her the truth because, well, that's what she wished Ben and Rachel had done for her, told her the truth.

"I found out something from Ben on Sunday, and you're going to be shocked. I was and I'm still shocked."

Abby sat up straighter and took a drink of her soda. "What?"

Jenna held her breath and then let it out slowly. "Ben was very sick last year. He had a bad heart, and he was dying. He's alive today because he received a new heart."

Abby's eyes grew wider. "He had a heart transplant?"

Jenna nodded. "Yes. He did."

Abby was quiet for a moment and then said, "He has Daddy's heart, doesn't he?"

Jenna nodded again. She waited for Abby to get angry, just like Jenna did, but instead, Abby looked thoughtful. "I can't believe he has Daddy's heart." She shook her head in wonder. "Daddy's heart is alive and beating in someone else's body. I knew that of course but it really didn't seem real. Like, it was possible that whoever got his heart died anyway, but he didn't and he's Ben." Abby looked at her mother quizzically. "Is that why y'all were fighting?"

"You heard us?"

Abby cocked her head. "I knew something was going on and then Ben left before the pizza came."

"He had known for a while and he never even told me. Rachel knew too." Jenna got up and threw her trash in the bin and then leaned against the counter. "I felt betrayed. That was something he should have told me the minute he found out."

Abby looked thoughtful. "Maybe he was scared."

"That's what he said, but he still should have told me." Jenna sipped her soda. "To be honest, I'm surprised you're taking this so well."

Abby shrugged. "Why would I be mad? It's not like he found out he had Dad's heart and then stalked you. That's not what happened, right? It was just a coincidence?"

Jenna rubbed her face, tired and exhausted. "No, he had no idea until I told him about what happened to your dad."

Abby stood up and threw her trash away and opened the cabinet to get some cookies out. "Maybe that's why you two had such a good connection. Katy and I noticed it the first time we saw you together at church. He kept staring at you and you kept trying to take a peek at him when no one was looking." She took a bite of cookie and looked thoughtful. "Isn't that something? Daddy's heart is still in love with you, Mama."

Abby left the kitchen and Jenna stood in shock. Was her daughter right? She did feel attracted and connected to Ben right from the start. She still remembered the first time she turned around and saw him in church. But why didn't he tell her and why was he scared? If Ben had told her as soon as he figured it out, would that really have made a difference? Would she still push him away? She remembered the look on his face when he left Sunday night. Thinking about it now made her feel ashamed. She didn't even give him a chance. She ordered him out the door because she was scared. She knew she was falling for Ben, and she was looking for the first excuse to bail because she didn't want to betray Craig and have people talk behind her back, just like her mother said. Elizabeth planted the seed, and it began to grow and grow, trying to choke out the love she felt for Ben. She did love Ben. She loved Ben. She had to let him know; but how?

Chapter 30

It was Saturday afternoon and Ben was on his way to the park. Rachel had asked him to meet her. She had some news about Jenna, but she didn't want to get into it over the phone. He'd had a horrible week. He felt better after he talked to Rachel Sunday night, but every day got worse when he never heard from Jenna. He talked to his doctor who informed him that it wasn't impossible, but it wouldn't be ideal for him to adopt without a partner. There was a lot of red tape and could take years. Ben wasn't giving up, though, and would do whatever it took. He wanted a child, and he had a lot of love to give. Whether it was a baby or older child, God would lead him in the right direction, he just had to have patience.

Ben began walking across the bridge that led to the park. He could hear children playing and the pitching sound of horseshoes. People were out in droves because it was sunny and beautiful. The usually humid air was dryer, which made it so much more pleasant. Ben stopped on the bridge that overlooked the river. Geese were sitting on the banks in the shade. He shaded his eyes and noticed a young boy fishing with his father on one of the small docks. Maybe that would be him one day. He continued walking and then sat down on one of the available benches surrounding the playground. Kids were running and shrieking, causing him to smile. One little girl, who looked about four years old, held a balloon filled with helium. She tripped and lost her grip on the string.

Ben jumped up and grabbed it before it could float up in the sky. He handed the balloon back to the little girl and her distressed frown turned into a smile. "Thank you."

Ben nodded and said, "You're welcome." She toddled off and Ben watched her until he saw a mother pushing her baby in a stroller. She was coming towards him on the asphalt path and Ben's eyes grew wide. It was Jenna and she was smiling shyly. He stood up, watching her intently, afraid it was a dream. She looked like an angel, her dark hair and blue eyes shining. He couldn't say anything; he could only watch her in wonder.

Jenna was the first to speak. "Hey, Ben."

He looked at a sleeping Sam in the stroller. "I guess Rachel's not coming?" Ben waived at the bench for Jenna to sit down and then sat down beside her.

Jenna shook her head. "No. Just me, and Sam, of course." She looked a little sheepish. "I asked Rachel to ask you to come here. I needed to talk to you, to explain the reason I acted like I did."

Ben tried to stop her. "Jenna, it's okay. I can't imagine the shock. I should have told you as soon as I..."

Jenna held up her hand. "No, Ben, I understand you were scared of how I would react. Rachel told me that you were scared I would be mad because Craig had to die for you to live, but that wasn't why I reacted the way I did. Craig was going to die anyway. It had nothing to do with you." Jenna took a deep breath and took Ben's hand and held it. "To be honest, I was falling for you, Ben, and I was scared. I felt guilty and I felt like I was betraying Craig. Mom gave me a hard time and said people would talk about me behind my back and my husband hadn't been in the grave for a year. When you told me about your heart, I grabbed that excuse to distance myself from you. It was wrong." Jenna squeezed his hand. "I love you, Ben. I know that now and I hope you can forgive me."

Ben brought Jenna's hand up to his lips and kissed her. "There's nothing to forgive." Ben pulled Jenna closer and wrapped his arms around her and hugged her. He closed his eyes and felt the warmth spreading through his body. "I love you, too. I have loved you before I even knew you."

Jenna's arms came around Ben too. "How can you love someone you never met?"

Ben pulled back and put his fingers on Jenna's chin. "I dreamed about you, Jenna. I dreamed about you and then I saw you in church that day. I thought I was still dreaming."

Jenna looked perplexed. "You dreamed about me before you met me?" She shook her head. "That's crazy."

Ben smiled. "I not only dreamed about you, but we were kissing in my dream."

Jenna's bottom teeth tugged on her lower lip, and she grinned. "Was it a good kiss?"

Ben's hands cupped Jenna's cheeks and he grinned back. "It was the best kiss I ever had, that is until I kissed you in the hospital parking lot. Now, that one topped everything."

Jenna looked at Ben expectantly. She raised her eyebrows and cocked her head. "Well, we could try and top that one."

Ben leaned down until his lips almost touched hers. "Right here in front of God and the whole town?" When Jenna nodded, his lips touched hers and then he thought he must be dreaming or in heaven or a little bit of both.

Chapter 31

"Okay, give me the scoop and give it to me now."

Jenna almost laughed at the expectant look on Rachel's face.

"Whatever do you mean?" She smiled to herself and continued drying the plate she had just rinsed. After their conversation in the park, Ben had followed Jenna back to her house where they had a late lunch. He had watched Sam while she fixed some sandwiches and then they sat on the living room floor, watching the baby play with his portable mobile. Ben left reluctantly, but not before they kissed a few times. Jenna still couldn't wipe the smile off of her face.

"You know what I mean." Rachel helped herself to some water from the fridge. "I know it's good, judging by the goofy smile on your face."

Jenna put the plate away and then turned to her friend who took a seat at the kitchen table. She fanned her face with her hand and then placed her hand on her chest, sighing. "First of all, he is an amazing kisser and I just want to let that be on the record."

Rachel nodded and then patted the kitchen chair, motioning Jenna to sit down. "Now you're talking. What else?"

Jenna took a deep breath. "Oh, Rachel, he is amazing. He's so incredibly sweet. You know what he told me?" She put her finger in her mouth and chewed on her nail nervously. "He told me he dreamed about me before he even met me. Is that not strange?"

"What do you mean?"

"He dreamed of me, and we kissed in his dream." Jenna shook her head in wonderment. "That's why he kept staring at me in church that first time, because he had already dreamed of me and then there I was. Is that even possible?"

Rachel shrugged. "I don't know, but I don't think he would make something like that up."

"I feel foolish even saying this, but is it because he has Craig's heart? Is that why he's having these dreams, I mean I could maybe see it if he had Craig's brain but that's not even possible, but his heart?"

"Does it even matter? You both have an obvious connection and attraction. Don't analyze it. Don't overthink it. Just be glad you have it. Not everybody does, especially twice."

Jenna began twisting the cloth place setting nervously. "I told him that I love him, and he said he loved me. I do love him, Rachel, but I still worry that we're moving too fast. When I'm with him, I don't think, I just act. And then later I'm second guessing myself."

"Well, quit thinking so much. Nobody says that you have to do anything right now. Just enjoy, Jenna. You deserve it. You've been through so much."

Jenna couldn't help but feel guilty. If she had died instead of Craig, would she want him to move on and be happy with someone else? She knew that she should want him to be happy, but just thinking about him with another person would break her heart. What if Craig was in heaven watching everything unfold? What if he was sad that she had already moved on to someone else?

After Rachel left, Jenna was getting ready for bed when she heard Abby come home. She walked into Abby's room, didn't see her, and then found her in Sam's room. She was standing over the crib watching the baby sleep, so Jenna walked up behind her and put her arms around her. "Are you okay?"

Abby turned in her mother's arms and hugged her. Jenna patted her and then said, "You want to talk about it?" Abby nodded and then they both walked out of the room and into Jenna's room.

They both got in the bed and Jenna patiently waited for her daughter to talk about whatever was bothering her. Abby cuddled up against her mother. "I had a long talk with Isaac today." Before she could continue, Chip jumped up on the bed, purring loudly. He settled cozily up between them. "He told me he's sorry that he's been distant. He said he feels overwhelmed, especially since he started college."

Jenna nodded. "That's understandable." Abby pulled a throw blanket up and Jenna pulled her closer and began stroking her hair.

"I love Sam."

When Abby didn't say anything else, Jenna said, "I know you do, sweetie."

"I love him, but I feel like I'm more of a sister than a mother."

Jenna sighed. "Abby, you're so young. I know you're overwhelmed too. It's okay. We'll get through this."

Abby turned towards her mother. "You're so much better with him than me."

"Abby, you're doing a great job. The older he gets, the more comfortable you are with him. It will get better, I promise."

"Mom, what if you were his mom instead of me?"

"What do you mean? You want me to adopt him?"

"You wouldn't have to adopt him, but you would be his mom instead of me."

Jenna shook her head. "If I'm going to raise him, honey, he would have to be mine legally. But I don't want you to make any rash decisions and do something that you would regret later."

"I've been thinking about it a lot. I even mentioned it to Isaac."

"What did Isaac say?"

"He said he's not ready to be a father, but his parents don't want him to relinquish his rights." Jenna wasn't surprised and since his parents were lawyers, they would always think ahead.

Jenna smiled. "Let's just take it one day at a time, Abby. This is not a decision to make without a lot of thought and prayer." Jenna's smile was only on the outside. On the inside, she began to worry that trying to raise Sam would not always be easy and simple.

Chapter 32

At work the following Monday, Ben had a bounce in his step and a smile on his face... that is until he got a text from Sarah. *Hey, Ben, is there any way I can meet with you this evening after work?* Ben groaned. What did she want now? When he didn't respond right away, she texted again. *I wouldn't ask but it's really important.*

Ben sighed. He didn't want her to come by his apartment, so he texted her to meet him at his mother's house at 6 o'clock. He also texted his mother to let her know that he was coming by and that Sarah wanted to meet him there to talk. Nancy called him right away.

"What in the world does she want to meet you about?"

"I don't have any idea. She just said it was important."

"She's up to no good."

Ben laughed. "Whatever she's up to, hopefully, won't last too long. Want me to bring some dinner?"

"No. I've already got a roast in the Crockpot. I was going to call you to let you know in case you wanted to come by, but I got distracted because Betty Green came over. We got to talking about the Marshalls that live at the end of the street, you know, the ones that haven't mowed their yard in forever? Well, anyway, Betty said that they're getting a divorce and that Mr. Marshall moved out and left poor Debbie and all those kids. They have 5 kids all under the age of 7. I just couldn't..."

Ben interrupted his mom. "Look, Mom, you can tell me all about it tonight. I've got a meeting in five minutes, and I need to get my material ready."

"Oh, I'm sorry. I'll tell you about it later. See you at 6."

"Bye, Mom." Ben hung up and began rubbing his forehead.

Brittany walked in with the files he requested. "Are you okay?"

Ben shook his head and laughed. "Mom."

Brittany laughed too. "Gotcha." She put the files on his desk. "The meeting has been delayed about 30 minutes, so you've got a little more time. I pulled all the specs you requested, and the updated contracts have been reprinted. I just need your signature on these." Brittany placed the contracts in front of him and handed him a pen.

Ben signed the papers and then handed them back to his secretary. "Thanks, Brittany. I don't know what I'd do without you."

She smiled. "I'm going to pick up some coffee in the shop downstairs. You want some? The usual?"

"That would be great." Ben pulled out his wallet and handed Brittany some cash. "Buy yours out of that too."

* * *

Traffic was a nightmare coming out of the city, so Ben was late when he pulled in his mom's driveway. Sarah's car was already there, and she was sitting with his mother on the porch rocking chairs.

Sarah was smiling but Nancy had a pinched look on her face.

"Hey, Ben! I was just telling your mom about my parent's anniversary party that's coming up. They've been married 50 years, so my sister and I decided to go all out. We're celebrating at Stowe Botanical Gardens and it's going to be awesome. I hope you both can come."

Nancy rolled her eyes as Ben stepped on the porch, so he knew what she thought about the invite.

"You know how Mom and Dad just adore you. I know it would just tickle them to death if you both came."

The last thing Ben wanted to do was go to his ex-wife's parent's anniversary party. "I just don't think that it's a good idea, Sarah."

"Don't say no, please just think about it. I'll be sending an official invitation in the mail." Sarah looked at Nancy. "Your mom's been telling me how wonderful you've been doing. I just can't believe how great you look. I'm so happy for you, Ben."

Ben leaned against the porch rail and crossed his arms. "Thank you. I feel like I'm back to my old self, finally. You okay?"

Sarah nodded but he could tell she was trying too hard. "I've been okay. Walk me to my car?" She stood and turned towards Nancy. "Thanks for the talk, Nancy. It was so good to see you." She leaned over and hugged his mom.

"I hope it all works out for you. I'll say a prayer." Nancy stood up. "I'm going to check on my roast. Dinner is almost ready, Benji."

Ben walked Sarah to her car. She stopped at the door and then turned towards him. "I was telling your mother that Kip and I broke up."

"Oh, wow, I'm sorry about that. Is everything okay?"

"Yes, I'm fine now. It's been a little crazy, but I knew that I would be making a mistake by marrying him. Kip is not taking it well."

"What do you mean?"

Sarah sighed. "He's a very jealous person and very possessive. To tell you the truth, he's been scaring me. I didn't mean to pour out all my problems like this. I really just wanted to let you know about the anniversary party, but I did think you needed to know that the wedding was off."

"How has he been scaring you?"

Sarah began biting her lip and then looked up, her eyes beginning to fill with tears. "He wouldn't leave me alone, so I stopped taking his calls. He leaves messages on my phone constantly. I've moved back in with my parents because I'm afraid to be alone. To be honest, I'm scared to death."

Ben didn't know what to say and then he froze when Sarah put her arms around his waist and hugged him. Not knowing what to do, he loosely put his arms around her and patted her back. "Have you notified the police?"

Sarah shook her head. "No, but Daddy said I needed to. I'm just so embarrassed."

Ben put his hands on her shoulders and gently pushed her away from him. "Your dad is right, Sarah." He opened her car door and motioned for her to get in. "I don't know this guy, but it's better to be safe than sorry."

Sarah sat down in the car and began crying. "I just don't understand how I could have been so stupid."

"You can't blame yourself for his behavior, Sarah."

"I'm not talking about that. I'm talking about me and you." She looked up at Ben with tears falling down her face and hope in her eyes. "Ben, I still love you." When Ben didn't say anything, Sarah told him, "You don't have to say anything. I know I messed up, but I couldn't let one more day go by without letting you know how I feel." She took a deep breath and smiled. "I know it's too late for us, but we can still be friends, right?"

Ben swallowed and then slowly nodded. "Of course. I am worried about you. You need to let the police know right away, okay?"

"I will, Ben. Thanks for listening." She shut the door and started the car. Before she put it in reverse, the window came down. "Please come to the party, Ben. It would mean so much to all of us."

Nancy's hands were on her hips when he walked into the kitchen. "I told you she's up to no good."

Ben grabbed a bottle of water out of the fridge and sat down at the table, taking a deep breath. He closed his eyes and shook his head. He really didn't know what to think of Sarah. There was a time when he would have been ecstatic to know that Sarah still loved him. He rubbed the evening stubble on his chin.

"She told you about the bad breakup and that he's stalking her?"

"Yep."

Nancy took the dish towel that was in her hand and threw it over her shoulder and sat down. "Ben, you know I don't like to get in your business, but you need to stay away from her. Women like Sarah are trouble."

Ben knew it was true, but he still questioned his mother. "How so?"

"How can you ask me that? She left you when she thought you were dying, Ben. And now that you're better and moving on, she wants you back."

"I know you're right, Mom." Ben got up and looked out the kitchen window. "I loved her so much and she broke my heart."

Nancy got up and put her arm around Ben. "If you get back together with her, believe me, she will break your heart again and again."

Ben nodded. "I know. I know that's true. Listen, I don't want to talk about Sarah anymore. How's that roast coming? It sure smells good."

Later that evening, Ben was sitting on his couch in his apartment watching television, but his mind was wandering back to what Sarah had told him. He pulled out his phone and looked at some pictures of him and Sarah in happier times. One was of Sarah, her hair blowing wildly on top of Grandfather Mountain. There was also one of them both smiling happily. His arm was around Sarah, and she was holding onto his other hand. He remembered the sweet older lady who offered to take their picture. She had told them that she had never seen a couple more in love.

Ben closed the phone and threw it on the couch. He did love her, he had loved her madly, but now he only felt melancholy for what they had shared. She threw it away and now he was past caring. He picked up the remote and began scrolling through the channels again, bored and frustrated. He heard his phone vibrating and almost didn't answer it, but in the end he did, and he was so glad.

"Hey, Ben."

Ben smiled just hearing her voice. "Jenna."

"I hope I'm not bothering you, but I just put Sam down and I just really wanted to talk to you."

"You're not bothering me at all. I'm glad you called. How is the little feller?"

"He's good. I think he's found his voice." Jenna chuckled. "He's been singing and cooing all evening."

"Did you have any trouble getting him down?"

"No, he was perfect. He's not fighting sleep like he used to and it's getting easier and easier."

"Good. I miss you."

"I miss you, too."

"When can I see you again?" Ben didn't want to sound so needy, but he missed Jenna, he missed Sam, and he even missed Abby. She was slowly warming up to him and it thrilled him. He didn't want just Jenna; he wanted the whole package. Things ended with Sarah for a reason and now he knew why.

"Well, I was wondering if you would like to come over for dinner Friday night?"

"Tell me what time and I'll be there. Can I bring anything?"

"Just yourself. Would 6 be too early? I know Friday afternoon traffic can sometimes be a little hectic."

"I'll be there if I have to leave work by noon."

Jenna laughed. "Okay, then. I guess I better go. Tomorrow is going to be a big day. I've got classes scheduled all day in the media center."

"Goodnight, Jenna."

"Goodnight, Ben."

"Sweet dreams." When Jenna didn't say anything, Ben said, "I hope you dream of me."

Ben was getting ready to hang up when Jenna whispered, "I already have."

"What were we doing?"

Jenna snickered. "I'll never tell, but you can use your imagination. Okay, I really gotta go now. Goodnight."

She hung up before Ben could reply, but he was grinning from ear to ear.

Chapter 33

J enna was a little nervous about dinner. She just hoped that Abby would behave. You never knew what she would do or say; it just depended on her mood. Jenna made a lasagna the night before, so all she had to do was prepare the salad and bread. Thankfully, Sam was being good. Abby was playing with him in the living room and also scrolling on her phone.

Jenna heard the doorbell ring, but she stayed in the kitchen and let Abby answer it. She checked on the bread, but it wasn't quite finished so she got the salad dressing out of the fridge and placed it on the table, all the while trying to hear what they were saying in the living room.

"Mom, Ben's here." Abby shouted like Jenna was outside and not in the next room.

Jenna wiped her hands on a kitchen towel and then walked out to greet Ben. "Hey! You're right on time."

"I left early and worked on some reports at home. Interstate 85 is getting worse, so I didn't want to take a chance in case there was a wreck or something." Ben walked over to where Sam was laying and bent down to pick him up. "Hey, little fella." Sam watched Ben seriously for a moment and then broke out in a wide grin. "There's my smile."

Jenna was looking at them both with a smile on her face until she noticed Abby watching her. Abby looked knowingly at her mother and rolled her eyes. Trying not to let Abby get to her, she said, "Abby, can you get the baby carrier and take it into the kitchen? Hopefully Sam will be okay while we eat."

Once she was gone, Ben winked at Jenna, causing her heart to flutter. "You look fantastic."

Jenna had gone shopping earlier in the week and bought a couple of new outfits. She had also had her hair trimmed and her roots touched up. "So do you." Before she could say anything else, Abby was back, chugging the carrier.

"Is there room on the table?"

"Yes. I'm going to leave the food on the stove." She motioned everyone to come in the kitchen and then got the bread out of the oven, placing it on a hot pad on the counter. "Y'all have a seat. I hope you like lasagna, Ben."

Ben carried Sam into the kitchen and placed him in the seat. "It's one of my favorites."

"I've got tea, water, and diet soda."

"Water is fine."

"Everyone, just help yourself." Jenna watched nervously as Abby and Ben filled their plates, and then she filled her own and sat down. She wasn't sure how to go about saying the blessing, wondering if she should say it or ask Ben, but he settled it for her.

"You want me to ask for the blessing?"

Jenna nodded. "Sure, that would be wonderful."

They all bowed their heads. "Dear Heavenly Father, we come to you tonight praising your Holy name. Thank you for this food and thank you for always being with us, leading and guiding us. Forgive us our sins. We ask these things in Jesus' name. Amen."

Jenna looked at Abby and they both grinned. Ben saw them and said, "What?"

"That sounded just like Daddy's blessing. He usually always said the same thing." Abby began eating while Jenna and Ben shared another smile.

Jenna picked at her food, too nervous to eat with gusto, but Ben ate as if he thought it was the best lasagna he ever had. "I'm not kidding, lasagna is one of my favorites. This is really good."

"Thank you. I'm glad you're enjoying it. It's my mom's recipe. We use cottage cheese instead of ricotta."

"I like yours better than Nana's, Mom. She doesn't put enough cheese on top." Abby took a bite of the bread and chewed thoughtfully. "Ben, why did you have to have a heart transplant?"

"Abby! That's kind of a rude question to be asking."

Ben wiped his mouth with his napkin. "I don't mind at all." He looked at Abby and said, "I had a heart defect that I had inherited from my father. He died at a young age, and I would have too if I hadn't gotten a new one."

"Does it feel weird having someone else's heart beating in your own body?"

Ben nodded. "Yes. It was really weird, but the longer I have it, the more I get used to it."

Jenna appreciated his candidness, but she didn't want him to feel distressed at the turn of their conversation. "Ben, Abby does not have a filter so if you don't feel comfortable, please don't feel like you have to answer." She looked pointedly at Abby. Sam began fussing so she put a pacifier in his mouth.

Undeterred, Abby went on. "I just want to say that it's really strange." She held up both of her hands, shrugging. "Ever since you met Mom, you seem to have a thing for her. Is it because you have Daddy's heart?"

Jenna looked upward as if she was asking for help from God.

Instead of being mad, Ben laughed out loud. "It's okay, Jenna, really." Taking his time answering, Ben finally said, "I'm not really sure, Abby. I do feel a definite connection with your mother, and you, too. Is it because of your dad's heart? Only God knows the answer to that question."

Abby looked satisfied with his answer. "Well, I like you, but you'll never be my daddy."

"Abby!" Jenna said warningly.

"I hear you loud and clear and I appreciate your honesty." Ben didn't seem offended and continued eating his dinner.

Abby looked at her mother smugly. "Katie called earlier and wanted to know if I could spend the night. I said I'd let her know later. Can I?"

Feeling exhausted from the tension, Jenna gave her assent. "As long as her parents are home."

Abby finished up her dinner and then got up to leave. Jenna hollered as she was headed to her room, "Text me when you get there."

Once she was gone, Ben laughed again. "Boy, she's a firecracker."

Jenna rubbed her temples. "You don't know the half of it."

Sam began crying earnestly so Jenna got up. "It's his bedtime. I guess I better get his bottle ready and put him to bed."

Ben got up too. "I'll heat the bottle. You go ahead and get him ready for bed. I'll bring it to you once it's ready."

Jenna smiled her thanks and carried Sam to his room. She did a quick wipe down and changed his diaper. His little arms and legs were getting chunky, and he would soon be outgrowing his sleepers. She made a mental note to get the larger sizes out of storage so she could wash them and get them ready for wear. Even his diaper was snug. Abby was petite, but Sam looked like he would take after his daddy. Isaac was tall, almost six feet and probably still growing. Both of his parents were tall too. Phillip and Renee had come over to see Sam a few times. Jenna knew it was only a matter of time before they decided they wanted to spend more time with their grandchild. Jenna appreciated the fact that they left most of the care to her and Abby, especially while he was an infant, but as he grew older, things would probably change. She decided that she would worry about that later.

Jenna put a zip-up sleeper on Sam and then sat down with him in the rocker. Ben came in holding the bottle. "I squirted a little on my hand and it's good to go. Can I feed him?"

Jenna got up and handed him the baby. "Okay, you feed him, and I'll read to him."

Looking like a pro already, Ben put the burp cloth on his shoulder. "You read to him already? Isn't he a bit young?"

"Maybe, but I like routines and he seems to like it. Abby usually feeds him while I read. The books are not very long, and I put a lot of inflection in my voice." Jenna walked over to the bookshelves on the wall and picked out one of her favorites. She sat down on the small bed and opened the book.

Jenna tried not to watch Ben watching her while she read about baby animals and their adventures on the farm. Sam finished his bottle before Jenna finished the story. Once she was done, Ben put Sam on his shoulder and patted him until he let out a loud burp. "Good grief, son. That's louder than some burps I've heard in the boys locker room."

Jenna giggled. "You should hear the other end." She stood up and turned off the lamp and then whispered, "Go ahead and put him down. I'll put the dishes in the dishwasher."

Jenna was almost finished when Ben came in the kitchen. All she had to do was wipe down the table. He stood in the doorway, leaning against the edge, watching her. "I can't believe how fast he goes to sleep."

"He usually doesn't have any problem going to sleep but staying asleep is a different issue. Sometimes he wakes up 20 times a night." She draped the dish cloth on the edge of the sink and then walked towards Ben. "Want to watch television?"

Ben nodded and then put his hand on Jenna's back as they walked towards the couch. They sat down next to each other, their legs lightly touching. Jenna picked up the remote from the coffee table and turned on the TV. "Anything you want to watch? I've got some shows that I've recorded." Jenna pulled up her recordings and Ben laughed. "What?"

"How many episodes of *Snapped* do you have?" Ben gave her a questionable look. "Is there something I need to know about you?"

Jenna smirked. "I'm a little obsessed with killer shows, I admit it." She tried to look innocent. "Is that a bad thing? A deal breaker?"

Before he could answer, Jenna's cell phone rang. When she saw who it was, she rolled her eyes. "It's Mom. I better get this." Jenna answered and wished she hadn't.

"Jenna, I just drove by your house on my way home from my art class and I saw a car in the driveway. Is that Ben's car?"

Jenna looked at Ben and smiled sheepishly. "Yes, Ben came over for dinner and we're watching television now."

"Do you think that's a good idea? If I noticed it, other people probably will too. They may think the worst of you, you follow?"

Jenna rolled her eyes dramatically. "I'm really not worried about other people, Mom. Ben and I are friends. It's nobody's business."

"Reputations are everything, Jenna. Please don't ruin yours."

Now Jenna was beginning to get perturbed. "Mom, please. I'm sure nobody cares. I love you but I'm going to say goodnight now. I'll talk to you tomorrow."

"I wouldn't say anything if I didn't care. I love you too. Goodnight."

Jenna took a deep breath and ended the call. "Moms." She shook her head. "You gotta love them."

Ben chuckled. "Yeah, even the best ones can drive you crazy."

Jenna picked up the remote again and scrolled down until she came to a *Dateline: Secrets Uncovered.* "Let's watch this, they're always real interesting." Ben nodded and they settled back on the couch, getting comfortable. Jenna's phone began vibrating so she paused the program before it even began. She looked at Ben and said, "Sorry, it may be Abby. She did text me earlier. Hopefully she's okay." She looked at her phone. "No, it's Rachel." Jenna laughed and then read Rachel's text.

Hope you're having fun. Don't do anything I wouldn't do. Wink, Wink. I'm at the restaurant. If you never hear from me again, tell my story and don't let the killer get away with it.

Ben looked perplexed. "What the heck does that mean?"

Jenna laughed. "She's been on this Christian dating site, and she has a date tonight." Jenna laughed out loud. "I wish you could hear about some of the dates she's been on. Hopefully her date tonight is not a serial killer or a dud." She picked up the remote again. "Okay, let's try this again."

As they watched the program, Chip meandered on the couch and finally settled on one of the throw pillows, purring so loudly Jenna had to turn the volume up. Jenna felt Ben's arm go around her shoulders and she smiled to herself. It was so nice having Ben around. She felt so safe and comfortable with him. His fingers were massaging her shoulder and then rubbed her neck. She closed her eyes, focusing on the warm, tingly feelings he was creating. She swallowed and then leaned forward just a bit. Ben's hands began ministering to her back. A small groan escaped her lips revealing just how good it felt as he kneaded and rubbed the tension away. Jenna began to realize just how dangerous having a man in your house could be. Maybe her mom was right. She stood up quickly and asked Ben if he wanted any popcorn. Ben stood up too, but instead of talking about popcorn, he turned Jenna toward him and bent down and kissed her before she even had time to react. Jenna moaned again causing Ben to kiss her even more thoroughly until her legs became wobbly and weak.

She didn't have sense enough to stop, but thankfully Ben did. He was breathing heavily and touched his forehead to hers. "I think I better go now." Jenna felt his lips on her forehead and wished he could stay but nodded instead. "Thank you for the great dinner. Next time, I want to take you out somewhere. Maybe Mom can watch Sam."

Ben took Jenna's hand as he walked towards the door. He put his hand on the doorknob but instead of opening it, he pulled Jenna into his arms and kissed her again. "Okay, I really gotta go now before I can't." He kissed her one more time on the forehead and whispered, "I love you, Jenna" and then he was gone.

Jenna dreamily walked back to the sofa and sat down. She pulled Chip close and hugged him. "Oh, my, Chip. He sure is a good kisser."

Chapter 34

"Thanks for coming by, Benji. The smoke detector has been beeping since noon and it's about to drive me up the wall." Nancy had called Ben at work and asked him to stop by. "Good thing I don't have Bonnie anymore. She would have shaken herself to death. She couldn't stand a beeping noise." Bonnie was his mom's Yorkshire Terrier that had died about two years before of old age. "I would have done it myself, but you always fuss when I climb on a ladder."

Ben began rummaging through the kitchen drawer for some batteries. "Where are the Double A batteries?"

"They're in there. Probably near the back of the drawer."

Once Ben found the right size batteries, he grabbed the step ladder that was leaning against the door frame and placed it below the smoke detector, which was emitting a very annoying beep. As he worked to replace the batteries, Nancy droned on and on.

"I talked to Jenna today. She thanked me for watching little Sam the other night. That baby is the sweetest. I think he's beginning to teethe a little. I was going through my pictures the other day looking at old baby photos of you and Laura and guess what I found? A little plastic box of baby teeth. I think even some of Bonnie's teeth were in there too."

Ben laughed. "Why in the world would you keep baby teeth, and especially Bonnie's teeth?"

Nancy shrugged. "I have no idea. I just couldn't bear to throw away anything. One day, you need to look at all that stuff. I'll never get Laura home long enough to go through it."

"What am I going to do with it?"

"I don't know. You may be interested in seeing your old report cards. I even have things you wrote in your journal." Nancy laughed. "I swear, you were so funny." Nancy could barely talk for laughing. "One time you wrote about seeing the neighbor's dog, Rex. Remember him? He was that huge overgrown puppy that liked to steal things out of everyone's yard, and you were scared to death of him. Apparently, you saw some boots in our yard, and you wrote that Rex must have scared the boots off of somebody." Nancy was laughing so hard, she had to sit down.

"Well, I'm glad you're so amused."

"There's more where that came from. You had a wonderful imagination, but you couldn't spell worth a flip."

"Still can't."

"Anyway, back to Jenna. She said she was coming by, too, with little Sam. I gave her the address. She should be here any minute. She wanted to bring by a gift. I told her she didn't have to give me anything, but she wouldn't take no for an answer."

Ben finished connecting the batteries and climbed down off the ladder. "Yeah, she told me she was coming by. I think we're going to go and grab a bite to eat." Ben thought about asking his mom if she wanted to come too but decided not to. He was being selfish, but he wanted Jenna and Sam all to himself. He hadn't seen her all week, but they talked and texted every day.

He folded the ladder up and was walking towards the laundry room when the doorbell rang. "I'll get it. It's probably Jenna." He set the ladder down in the hallway and then opened the door, smiling, but it wasn't Jenna. It was Sarah. "Hey."

Sarah had her hand up like she was getting ready to knock on the door. "I didn't hear the bell, so I was getting ready to knock." She stood awkwardly and then finally said, "I decided to personally bring your invitations to Mom and Dad's anniversary party. I already stopped by your apartment but obviously you weren't there. I thought I might as well bring Nancy's."

Ben walked out on the porch instead of inviting her in. "You didn't have to do that. You could have mailed them."

Sarah took a deep breath. "I didn't mind." She swallowed and tried to smile but bit her lip instead.

Ben knew something was wrong. Instead of thanking her like he should so she would be on her merry way, he ended up asking, "Are you okay? Anything wrong?"

That was all the encouragement Sarah needed. "Oh, Ben, it's been an absolute nightmare." She leaned against the porch railing, placing her hand on her mouth anxiously. "Kip came to my house and he..." Sarah closed her eyes. "He pushed his way into the house, and he threatened me. He put his hands around my neck and shoved me against the wall." Tears filled her eyes and began slowly rolling down her face. "He said... he said awful things about me and that it would be so easy to snap my neck in two. I just knew he would do it, too, but at the last minute he let me go and left. I called my parents, and they came by and called the police, but they said there's really nothing I can do except put a restraining order against him, which I did."

"I thought you said you were staying with your parents."

"I was but I hadn't heard anything for a few days, and I wanted to take care of some things. He must have been watching me, waiting for me to go home." Sarah stepped up closer to Ben. "What am I going to do, Ben? I'm so scared."

Ben didn't know what to do or say. He hated that she was going through this nightmare but there was nothing he could do. As he was contemplating the situation, Sarah put her arms around him, shaking and crying. "I didn't mean to unload on you, but I needed a friend right now and you're the first person I thought of."

Ben stood awkwardly, still not knowing what to say or do. That was the way Jenna found them as she pulled next to the curb in front of his mother's house. He gently pushed Sarah away. "I'm sorry, Sarah. I wish I could help you, but I can't."

Sarah noticed Jenna and looked curiously. "Who's that?"

"That's my girlfriend."

Chapter 35

Jenna was on her way to Nancy's house when Rachel called her cell. "I wanted to check on you. Are you okay?" It was the one-year anniversary of Craig's death, and Jenna had been morose all day. She was doing anything and everything to get her mind off the significance of the day. She couldn't believe that it had been a year already since her life changed forever.

"I'm okay. I'm on my way to Nancy's house to drop off a thank you gift and meet Ben—anything but sit at home." She had mixed feelings about meeting Ben, like she was betraying Craig, but she knew that she was just being silly.

"I forgot to tell you at school that Michael wants to go out again Friday night."

"Really? That's awesome!" Rachel had had a surprisingly good time on her recent date. He was a science teacher in Charlotte, and they had a lot in common. Knowing that Rachel was so picky, Jenna didn't hold out much hope that the date would go well, but hearing the happiness in her best friend's voice proved otherwise. "I definitely want to hear all about it. Can I call you tonight?"

"Sure! Have fun and I'll talk to you soon."

Jenna had programmed Nancy's address into her phone, but she already had a good idea how to get there. She looked at Sam via the mirror, who was contentedly sucking on his pacifier. She had bundled him up in a thick sleeper because the weather had turned a little cooler. The leaves were just beginning to change and with the sun shining brightly; it was a beautiful fall day. Fall was her favorite time of the year. She loved the brisk coolness, the vibrant colors, and the earthy smell. Her mother dreaded winter and in turn dreaded fall because it brought on the winter. She said the shorter days depressed her, but Jenna looked forward to it. She loved turning on the gas logs and curling up by the warm heat. She would read a book or watch a movie, drinking tea or coffee. Usually, Craig had been busy with football during the fall, so she was left to fend for herself most of the time.

Jenna found the street and then the house, so she pulled up next to the curb. She checked on Sam and then released her seatbelt. Once she turned to get out of the car, she saw Ben on Nancy's porch. She was shocked to see a girl with her arms around him. She was so surprised that she froze, not knowing what to do. Ben gently pushed the girl away and then walked towards Jenna's car. He looked disconcerted and uncomfortable. Jenna's trance was broken when Sam let out a cry.

Hearing the baby cry, Ben walked to the passenger side and opened the car door, releasing Sam's seatbelt and pulling him out. "What's the matter, Sam?" Sam immediately stopped crying and gurgled happily.

Jenna got out of the car and stood awkwardly until Ben came back around. Ben spoke quietly. "I'm sorry about that, Jenna. That's Sarah, my ex-wife. I'll tell you about it later but let me introduce you first." Jenna nodded and walked with Ben to the porch. Sarah was smiling but Jenna could tell she was a bit tense. "Sarah, I want you to meet Jenna, my girlfriend." Ben turned to Sam and smiled. "And this is Sam."

Jenna held out her hand and Sarah shook it, but very lightly. "It's nice to meet you." Jenna tried to keep her hand from shaking. She couldn't believe this was Ben's ex-wife. She was so young and beautiful. Jenna felt old and plain standing next to her, exactly like the grandmother she was.

Sarah put her finger beneath Sam's chin. "It's nice to meet you, too, and look at this sweet baby. He's absolutely adorable."

Jenna noticed that Ben didn't clarify that Sam was her grandbaby and she decided not to as well. "Thank you."

Sarah then put her hands on her hips and cocked her head. "Ben, you didn't even tell me you had a girlfriend." She looked at Jenna. "This is so surprising, and you have a baby, my goodness."

Jenna smiled and then looked at Ben, who smiled back, taking his free arm and wrapping it around Jenna. "We haven't been dating all that long."

"I was just giving Ben and Nancy their invitations to my parent's anniversary party. I was over the other day but wanted to hand deliver the invites. My parents just adore Ben." Sarah turned and completely ignored Jenna, asking, "You and Nancy are coming to the party, aren't you? It wouldn't be complete without you."

Ben shook his head. "I told you before, Sarah, that it's not a good idea. I'm just going to leave it at that."

Jenna could see that Sarah was not used to being told 'no' and that she would be relentless until Ben said yes. She was unnerved, so she reached for the baby. "I'll take Sam inside. I need to give Nancy something. It was nice to meet you." She left them on the porch and walked inside just to find Nancy close to the door. She motioned for Jenna to come into the kitchen.

"Here, give me the baby. You don't look so good." Nancy placed Sam on her hip. "Sit down and I'll get you a drink. Water?" When Jenna nodded, Nancy grabbed a bottle out of the fridge and put it on the table. "I am so sorry you had to see that." Nancy sat in one of the kitchen chairs and placed Sam in her lap. "That girl is trouble and that's all I'm going to say about that."

Jenna took a drink of her water. "I don't know what I was expecting but it wasn't that."

Nancy nodded. "Yes, she's a beautiful girl—on the outside."

Jenna noticed that Nancy emphasized the word 'outside,' but before she could respond, Ben walked into the kitchen. He appeared concerned and pensive. He looked from Jenna to Nancy. "Everything okay in here?"

Nancy rolled her eyes. "That sure was some kind of show Sarah put on out there. I would have stepped outside and joined the party, but I didn't want to get my feet dirty."

If Jenna wasn't so upset, she would have laughed at Nancy. Ben continued to look uncomfortable. "Mom, can you watch Sam for a minute while I talk to Jenna?" After Nancy gave her consent, Ben held his hand out to Jenna and then pulled her to her feet. "We'll be back shortly."

They walked quietly outside and sat on the porch rockers. Ben took a deep breath. "I'm so sorry about that. I wasn't expecting her to show up."

Jenna sniffed. "It's okay, Ben. We're not married, and I don't own you." And then, "I had no idea how beautiful she was, and young."

Ben moved his chair closer to Jenna's. He took her hand and rubbed his thumb on her knuckles. "Jenna, she's not half as pretty as you. I don't want to talk about my ex-wife anymore. I want to know if you're okay. I know that today must have been hard for you."

Jenna never mentioned to Ben that it had been a year since Craig died, but of course he knew. It was a year ago today that he received Craig's heart. Big tears filled her eyes and she tried with all of her might not to cry, but the tears fell down her cheeks anyway. She was an emotional wreck and seeing Ben with Sarah was the final nail in the coffin. She wiped her eyes with her free hand. "I'm okay. Really." She laughed, but her tears told a different tale.

Ben pulled Jenna to her feet and wrapped his arms around her. "You're not okay, obviously." A sob escaped her lips and embarrassed her, but Ben only held her tighter. Jenna gave in and let Ben hold and console her, and eventually she began to feel calmer. He took her face in both hands. "I love you, Jenna. You know that, don't you?"

Jenna nodded, her eyes still glistening. He bent down and gently kissed her lips. "I have thought of no one and nobody since I met you, no, since I dreamed of you." He smiled when Jenna smiled. "If I thought you were ready, I would take you to the courthouse at the first available moment and marry you." He pulled her close again. "Because, Jenna, I do want to marry you. I want to be with you for the rest of our lives; you, Sam, and even Abby."

Jenna giggled. "You really must love me then."

Ben put his hands on Jenna's shoulders. "I know I'm supposed to wait until I have a ring and be in a more romantic setting other than my mom's front porch, but, hey, this feels right." He stepped back and got down on his knee looking up at Jenna. "Will you marry me, Jenna? I can wait as long as you need to."

Jenna was shocked. The last thing she expected today was a proposal. She had to admit that being married to Ben had crossed her mind, but it was something to be considered in the future—not now, not this soon. But just like Ben said, it did feel right. She wanted to marry him. She wanted to be with him all the time. She looked at him with all the love she had and nodded because she was so choked up that she couldn't utter a word. She had already been married to her soul mate, but thankfully God decided to give her another one.

Apparently she didn't need to speak because Ben pulled her up and gave her the biggest bear hug that just about knocked the breath right out of her.

They hugged and kissed until they both saw Nancy in the living room window. She was bouncing Sam on her hip and giving them a thumbs up, grinning from ear to ear. She shouted, "Come on in! Let's celebrate!"

Chapter 36

"What do you mean you're getting married?" Elizabeth sat down in the kitchen chair as if her whole body had deflated. "Have you not listened to a word I've said?" She put her elbow on the table and then propped her chin on her fist.

Jenna mentally counted from 1 to 5 and then sat down opposite her mother. "I heard you, Mother, but you did what you had to do. Now let me do what I have to do."

"You have to marry Ben? Already?"

"Yes! I love him and I want to marry him as soon as possible." Jenna tried her best to make her mom understand. "We want to be together now, and we don't want to wait."

"What do you mean, now?"

"We want to have a Christmas wedding; nothing big, just the family and a few close friends. I've already talked to the minister, and we've set aside the Friday night before Christmas."

"Oh my Lord, this is unbelievable. I just don't understand it." She shook her head and closed her eyes as if in pain.

Jenna had talked to Ben, and they decided it would probably be best if she told her mother by herself. Jenna knew she wouldn't take it well and didn't want to put Ben through all the drama. Jenna had also decided to finally tell Elizabeth about Ben having Craig's heart.

"I have something else to tell you too, Mom."

Elizabeth looked up sharply. "What else could you possibly lay on my shoulders?"

Jenna braced herself. "Ben had a heart transplant."

Looking puzzled, Elizabeth said, "Is he in bad health? Are you afraid he's going to die and that's why you're rushing?"

Jenna shook her head. "No, Mom. He's doing really well. He said he had some problems at first but now he's doing great." Jenna looked intently at her mother. "He has Craig's heart."

"What?"

Jenna knew it was a shocker. Jenna and Ben had recently revealed the news to Craig's parents. Once the shock wore off, Lynn and Bill got excited and wanted to feel Ben's heart beating. Lynn could not stop hugging Ben.

"I checked with the hospital, and they confirmed that it's true. Craig's heart is alive and beating in Ben's chest, but that's not why I'm marrying Ben. I love him, Mother, and we've had a connection long before either one of us knew. I tried to fight it at first, but my love for him is too strong." Jenna reached for Elizabeth's hand. "Please try and understand, Mom."

Instead of taking Jenna's hand, Elizabeth jumped up out of her seat. "Have you gone mad?"

Jenna groaned. She knew it wouldn't be easy, but could her mother just once let her live her life without judgment and persecution?

Before she could say anything, Abby walked into the kitchen with Sam on her hip. "Nana, give Mom a break. It's not like she's marrying an axe murderer or something."

Elizabeth harrumphed. "Well! So, you're just fine and dandy with this, missy? You, 17, unmarried, and a black baby on your hip? You've both gone off the deep end and I have had just about all I can take. I've tried to be a good example for you both and live my life without blemish, but see what good it did me?"

Jenna stood up in anger when she saw her daughter's face drain of all color. "How dare you! Who are you to judge us?"

Elizabeth jabbed her finger at her chest. "I'm your mother and it's my job to guide you to make good choices in life, but I have failed miserably." By this time, Sam was whimpering and visibly upset. Elizabeth grabbed her pocketbook and walked to the kitchen door. Before she opened it, she turned to Jenna and Abby. "I don't even know what else to say to you since you don't listen, obviously. I'm going home."

Jenna immediately went to Abby and pulled her and Sam into her arms. "Honey, I am so sorry about that. Please don't pay attention to anything she said. She's upset and not thinking." Sam began crying earnestly so Jenna took him from Abby and held him closely, protectively.

Abby sat down in one of the kitchen chairs as if stunned. "How could she be so mean?"

Jenna didn't know what to say to help her daughter. She was stunned too. How could her mother be so cruel and hateful? Would they always be trying to protect Sam from small-minded people? He was innocent and a blessing and Jenna would always be thankful for him no matter what his skin color was. "Nana is not thinking clearly. Once she calms down, she'll realize what she's done, and she'll be so sorry that she hurt you."

Abby's head hung pitifully. "Mom, I loved Isaac and I still do. I never really thought about his skin color, but seeing others look at Sam differently has opened my eyes to how mean some people can be."

Jenna's heart was breaking for her child. She looked at Sam and smiled. "All we can do is love him and give him the best that we have to give. We can't help what other people say or do, and we definitely can't worry about it either. We can pray, though."

Abby sniffed. "How can we pray if we can't change the way people think?"

Jenna stood up and placed Sam on her hip. If she was going to have a deep discussion, she needed more coffee. After she poured a cup and put some milk and sugar in it, she sat back down. "We can always pray for others, Abby. We can pray for their understanding and compassion.

You never know what that person has been through. For example, your nana did not have the best childhood and that's affected her life and one of the reasons she's so controlling."

Abby knew that Elizabeth had a stepmother, but Jenna had never given her any specifics and it was something Elizabeth never talked about. Jenna only knew because of her aunt Peggy. Their mother died when Elizabeth was only 5 years old. Their father remarried rather quickly because he had several children, and he needed help raising them. Linda had two children of her own and needed a husband to help support them. The problem was that Linda was a very nasty and spiteful person, as were her two daughters. When Elizabeth's father was working or away from their home, Linda and her two daughters made her new husband's children miserable. Elizabeth vowed that she would never remarry and put her daughter through that. She also grew up in a very different era and time where whites married whites and blacks married blacks. One of her very good friends was a black woman who also volunteered at the hospital, so Elizabeth would never admit to being a racist.

Jenna tried to explain her mother's background to Abby. "I'm not excusing her, Abby, but I'm just trying to explain the way she is. We need to pray for her too. I know she'll come around. She loves you and she absolutely adores Sam. I've seen that with my own eyes."

Abby got up and walked over to Sam, reaching her arms out. "I don't know, Mom. I don't think I can ever forget this. Nana will have to change a lot if she ever wants to see my child again."

Jenna sighed. She couldn't blame Abby for being upset. Heck, Jenna was upset, but she knew how her mother was and how she often lashed out without thinking. Jenna loved her mother, though, and she had faith that her mom would come around, once again.

Chapter 37

Ben couldn't believe that he was finally going to marry Jenna. They decided that it would be silly to sell her house, so Ben would be moving in with them, which was fine by him. He loved her small house. It was cozy and warm and perfect. Ben looked around the gloomy apartment that he had never tried to make a home, glad he would never have to come back. After Christmas, they were flying to the Keys for some sun and relaxation. He was taking a few days off, and Jenna would still be on her Christmas break from school. Rachel and his mother were going to take turns staying with Abby so they could help with Sam.

He nervously checked his tie once again. Jenna's mother was still being obstinate and refused to come to the wedding. He prayed that she would change her mind. Ben didn't want to be the cause of any dissension between them. It was the only blemish on an otherwise perfect day. He checked his watch, but it was still too early to head to the church. His best friend, Mark, had already been by. They had talked about anything and everything until he had to leave to pick up his wife, Lucy, Daniel, and Hannah. Mark said he would see him at the church, and he would have the rings ready. Ben and Jenna had picked out the wedding bands just a week before. They had also picked out her engagement ring. He apologized for not giving it to her in the traditional way or by some elaborate way that could be filmed and posted on social media. He knew Jenna wouldn't want that anyway.

Ben looked at all of the boxes piled up in the living room. They contained mostly clothes, a few dishes, and some miscellaneous items. His sister, Laura, had helped him pack everything a couple of days before. She was here for the week and Nancy couldn't have been more excited. They had mostly been on their best behavior with only a few squabbles. Nancy just couldn't help herself when hinting and downright begging Laura to move back to North Carolina. She had all kinds of excuses, like Laura needed to get out before the next major earthquake knocked the whole state of California off the map. Laura would also have the advantage of being able to flush her toilet every time she used it, which was a major bonus in Nancy's opinion. She had also made a list of some possible candidates for Laura to date while she was in. Her neighbor, Betty, had a sister that had a nephew that had a cousin. Ben was proud of Laura for not going off on Nancy in a major way, which he knew she wanted to if all the eye rolling was any evidence.

Laura was crazy about Jenna, Abby, and Sam. Abby was very impressed that she was an assistant to a big movie executive. She wanted to know everything, but mostly the things that the public wasn't privy to. They were already planning a trip where Abby would come out and visit. All of a sudden, she wanted to be an actress in the worst way and was planning to take every drama course available at school.

Sarah was a little miffed that he didn't show up at her parent's anniversary party. She was a lot miffed when she found out Ben was getting married. In her own subtle way, she wanted to know why he would want to marry someone with a biracial baby. Nancy took every opportunity to praise Jenna in front of Sarah, which was funny to watch. After getting nowhere with Ben, Sarah finally gave up and moved on. Ben never heard anything more about Kip. He wondered if what she told him about Kip was all a big exaggeration.

Ben checked his reflection in the mirror and swiped at some lint on his suit. It was a little early, but he decided to head to the church anyway because he just couldn't wait anymore. Knowing that Jenna would be his wife in a few hours made him feel happy and content in a way he never thought possible, especially a year ago. He looked up and smiled, tears gathering in his eyes, and he thanked God.

Chapter 38

J enna was in one of the Sunday School rooms getting ready for the wedding. She had a simple ice blue dress that fit her to perfection. It cost more than she really wanted to pay, but it was beautiful and perfect. She hoped Ben would like it. She was sitting in front of a mirror touching up her makeup when Rachel walked in with the bouquet. Jenna didn't want to make a fuss, but Rachel insisted on picking out flowers. They were beautiful, of course, because Rachel had a knack for things like that, much more than Jenna did. After looking at the flowers and smiling gratefully, Jenna's face fell when she saw the worried look in Rachel's eyes.

"What's the matter?"

Rachel laid the bouquet on one of the tables. "I just wanted to warn you that your mother just pulled in the parking lot. I ran in as fast as I could to warn you."

Jenna sighed. "Really? Rachel, I swear, if she tries to ruin our wedding day..."

Rachel walked towards the door, peeped down the hallway and then jumped back inside the room, quickly closing the door. "Darn. She caught me. Boy, that woman is fast."

Knowing it was inevitable, Jenna walked towards the door, opening it before Elizabeth could knock. Jenna didn't say anything but looked at her mother with apprehension. Elizabeth unexpectedly smiled. "Jenna, can I talk to you?"

Jenna nodded and moved away from the door so Elizabeth could come in. Rachel started to leave but Jenna and Elizabeth both said, "Stay!" so Rachel stopped in her tracks and looked from one to the other, her eyebrows raised.

Elizabeth cleared her throat, still clutching her purse. "First of all, I want to apologize for the way I acted. I've been miserable knowing I caused you pain." Jenna was speechless, because hearing an apology from her mother was very rare. She was definitely surprised but pleasantly so. The next words out of her mouth were even more bewildering. "I've been doing a lot of soul searching, and I have come to realize that I have a big, fat mouth, and I need to learn how to keep my trap shut. I have no business trying to tell you how to live your life. You can marry today with my blessing and know that I love you, and Abby and Sam, with all my heart."

By the end of Elizabeth's speech, Jenna's mouth was wide open. Jenna didn't say anything; she just walked into her mother's waiting arms, crying tears of joy. They both cried silently until Rachel exclaimed, "I never thought you had it in you, Mrs. Johnston. I take it all back."

Elizabeth looked over Jenna's shoulder at Rachel. "Take what back?"

"Believing you were the most stubborn, hard-headed woman I ever knew. You follow?" Cluck cluck.

Rachel could hear Jenna snickering, but Elizabeth was oblivious to the inside joke. "I didn't mean to be, Rachel. I was just trying in my own way to help Jenna, but I realize now that I was terribly wrong." Elizabeth looked at her daughter. "Do you forgive me, sweetheart?"

Jenna hugged her mother even tighter. "Yes. Thank you so much, Mama. This means the world to me."

Jenna still couldn't believe it, but she had a wedding to get ready for. After she fixed her makeup again, she sat down so Rachel could brush her hair out and add a few soft curls. They all looked up as Abby walked in with Sam on her hip, but as soon as she saw her grandmother, she turned to leave.

"Hold on a minute, Abby. I need to tell you something." Elizabeth had to chase Abby to the door. "Please, honey, I want to apologize."

Abby stopped abruptly. "I don't want to hear it, Nana. You're a racist—plain and simple. I don't think there is anything you can say to me that will make me forgive you." Abby walked out of the door stubbornly, not looking back.

Elizabeth was visibly shaken. Jenna tried to console her mother, but Elizabeth shook her head. "I deserve that. I know I do."

"She had no right to talk to you like that." Jenna patted her mother's back. "I'll say something to her."

Elizabeth seemed to wake from her shock. "You most certainly will not. It's my mess, and I'll do what I need to do to convince Abby that I'm truly sorry. Don't you worry about a thing." Elizabeth turned to Rachel. "Make sure she gets ready. I'm going now. I'll see you at the ceremony."

After her mother left, Jenna and Rachel looked at each other in amazement. Both were shocked at the turn of events, not believing Elizabeth would ever stoop to apologizing or admitting that she was wrong. Rachel grabbed a can of hairspray, spraying Jenna's hair lightly. "What we have just witnessed today is a miracle. And it will also be a miracle if I make it through the day with this underwear creeping up my butt. Next time, I don't care if I have panty lines."

Jenna laughed. "There won't be a next time, I promise you." And then more thoughtfully, "You think Abby can get over this?"

Rachel shrugged. "Who knows? Abby is almost as stubborn as her Nana, but Elizabeth sure did surprise us. Maybe Abby will too."

"I hope so, but I'm not going to worry about that right now." Jenna giggled. "Can you believe I'm getting married again?"

Rachel sat down in one of the cold, metal Sunday school chairs. "Are you ready for tonight?" Ben had reserved a suite in one of the posh hotels in downtown Charlotte for the following two nights. Christmas Eve was the following Monday. Rachel grinned. "Just don't be making all kinds of loud noises, embarrassing me."

Jenna turned red. "Cut it out." Jenna stood up and checked for any creases marring her new dress. "I'm sure it will be just great."

Rachel gave her friend a perplexed look. "You didn't exactly sound convincing."

Biting her lip, Jenna tried to explain. "Well, he does have a new heart, so I guess he can do things like that...that uhhh...that require a level of...a level of excitement and such."

Rachel busted out laughing and then more seriously, "Are you worried about that?"

"Among other things."

"What other things?"

Jenna covered her face with embarrassment. "He has Craig's heart. Isn't that kind of weird? I just can't explain it."

"Some things just can't be explained, my friend. Sort of like graffiti on a train. You can't read it, but it's beautiful all the same, in its own weird sort of way."

"Are you comparing my honeymoon to train graffiti?"

Rachel shook her head 'no' and then nodded. "Yes, I guess I am. Just have fun and be creative, and it will be beautiful in its own sort of way."

Jenna groaned. "You are so weird. I don't know why I put up with you."

Rachel took her hand and smiled. "Because you love me as much as I love you. By the way, I'm so happy for you and Ben. He's such a great guy." She looked thoughtful. "He doesn't poop in buckets or drink too much or sneeze real loud in your ear. He's a real catch!"

Jenna grinned. "I know. So, when are you getting married?"

It was Rachel's turn to groan. "Uh, no time soon, thank you very much. Michael's a great guy but we're not even close yet. He is definitely a lot of fun, appreciates my weirdness unlike some people, and he's pretty hot to boot, but after that first bozo I was married to, I would never jump into marriage before I'm ready." Rachel walked towards the door. "Okay, it's time to go. You sure you want me to walk you down the aisle?"

Jenna held her hand out. "Absolutely, but first I want you to pray with me." They both bowed their heads as Jenna and Rachel took turns praying for her marriage to Ben. "Okay, let's go."

Chapter 39

Ben was trying to keep it together as he waited for Jenna to make her entrance. He was surprised and a little confused to see Elizabeth and Abby sitting beside each other, seemingly happy and ready for the wedding. God had definitely performed a miracle already and he hadn't even married Jenna yet.

Ben felt a tap on his shoulder and turned to his best man, Mark. Mark held out his hand, dropping the rings in Ben's hand. "Congratulations, Ben. She looks beautiful."

Ben turned quickly and watched as Jenna and Rachel began to slowly walk down the aisle. His emotions bubbled up, threatening to spill over and embarrass him. By the time Jenna got to his side, tears had gathered in his eyes, but he held himself in check. She was so beautiful and the smile on her face warmed his heart. Rachel gave him a funny look and then winked, whispering, "She's all yours now." Ben grinned as Rachel placed Jenna's hand in his and stood next to her during the ceremony, performing double-duty.

He couldn't believe he was marrying Jenna, this girl of his dreams. She was everything he wanted in a wife and more, and he promised to cherish her for the rest of his days. By the time Preacher Jennings pronounced them man and wife, Ben felt that his mind had wandered so much that he missed some of the vows, but it didn't matter. He vowed to himself and God that he would do anything and everything to take care of Jenna and make her the happiest wife on earth.

Ben finally kissed Jenna, noticing her eyes were wet and glistening as well. He took her hand and walked down the aisle and into the vestibule, having just a moment before the small group of friends and family came to wish them well. Ben kissed Jenna again quickly. "Hello, Mrs. Thompson." He then kissed her hand before placing it on his heart. "You have just made me the happiest of men."

Jenna blushed. "Your heart is beating so fast."

"My heart is happy and thankful for second chances."

Jenna moved closer and placed her cheek on Ben's chest. "I love you, Ben Thompson, and I am so thankful for second chances, too."

Epilogue

Rachel continued her correspondence with her son until she was finally able to meet him in person. He said he had never been mad at her. He loved his adoptive parents and had a very happy childhood. He really only wanted to meet her initially so he could find out his health history, but after meeting Rachel, they hit it off—as Rachel said, like shrimp and grits. She really liked her new boyfriend, Michael, or 'the science guy,' as she dubbed him.

Nancy was so happy, she was dancing for joy. Sam was the highlight of her life. She babysat every chance she got and then asked for more. Sam was in love with her, too, and when he was finally able to talk, he called her Nassie. She tried to correct him and wanted him to call her Gigi like all the cool grandmas, but Sam insisted on Nassie so Nassie it was.

Elizabeth stayed true to her word and gave her blessings to her daughter's marriage. Jenna wasn't privy to the conversation that Elizabeth had with Abby before the wedding but was thankful that her mom and daughter were able to get past the 'incident.' Being called a racist shocked Elizabeth, and she promised everyone she would do better.

Sam was a little spoiled. With so many grandparents, he had them all wrapped around his little finger. Isaac's parents were spending more time with him as he grew older but promised Jenna that they, along with Isaac, had no plans to seek custody of him. They just wanted to be a part of his life. Everyone, including Abby, wanted Jenna and Ben to formally adopt Sam. Sam would always know who his birth parents were but would call Jenna and Ben 'Mommy and Daddy.'

After being hot and cold with Ben at first, Abby began to warm up to him more and more. She said she couldn't help but feel guilty for loving Ben because she didn't want her daddy to ever think she forgot him for one minute. The day Ben jokingly called her 'Abby Lou Lou' was a turning point. She just knew her dad was giving her his blessing.

Jenna was happy. She would never forget Craig and the special love they shared, but Craig was gone. Ben turned out to be an unexpected bonus. Being a recipient of a heart transplant didn't guarantee that he would live a long life, but she would cherish every year, every day, every minute, and every second of being with him. Being without him wasn't an option.

Chip was happiest of all, except when Sam pulled his tail, or ear, or leg.

Acknowledgments

There are so many people I would like to thank for their support.

Thank you, Janie Jessee at Jan-Carol Publishing for taking a chance on me. I still can't believe it!

Kenny Bruce, my wonderfully talented husband, edits my work and gives me loads of insight. I tell him all the time, "I don't know what I don't know!" He encourages me and loves me for reaching my goals.

Thank you Deborah Corn, Blakeley Lewis, and Wanda Sheppard, for being the first to read this book. Your reassurance and support mean the world to me and give me the courage to keep on going. Also, thank you Carol Williams and Ladonna DeCaterina for being wonderful friends that will read my work and give me such inspiring feedback.

Thank you to Becky Ford, who always makes me laugh and gives me lots of inspiration.

Thank you to all my friends and family for your kind words and praise. It warms my heart and gives me the strength to keep on going and wanting to do my very best.

Thank you to my son, Adam, and his wife, Tif, for using your wonderful talent in creating my website, karengbruce.com. Your help and patience are greatly appreciated.

Thank you to my son, Sam, and his wife, Catherine, for reading my last book, *Josie: A Story of Forgiveness* (out loud), together. I'm sorry that I made you blush, Sam, and that you had to read some parts with a funny voice to keep from being embarrassed to death.

Thank you to my church family at Victory Baptist Church, in Bristol, Virginia. Your amazing support and love have been phenomenal.

My dad left this world in March 2022. I know that he is in heaven watching over me and my stepmother Evelyn. We miss you, Daddy.

Thank you most of all to my Father, in Heaven, who gives me the words and vision that I aspire to. I give Him all the praise and glory.

About the Author

Karen Bruce is married to Kenny Bruce. They live on a farm in Mendota, Virginia. They have two children and two grandchildren. Karen is also the author of *Josie: A Story of Forgiveness*.

You can contact Karen by email, karengbruce85@gmail.com, or on Facebook/Instagram (Karen G. Bruce), or at www.karengbruce.com.

Coming Soon

Carly: A Story of Redemption,
sequel to *Josie: A Story of Forgiveness*

The best thing that ever happened to Carly as a child was when her parents divorced. Things were never normal, but she learned to cope with their arguments and hostility, that is, until her father murdered her mother.

www.ingramcontent.com/pod-product-compliance
Lightning Source LLC
Chambersburg PA
CBHW030330020726
47493CB00004B/1217